For Gwen,

Love Finds a Way...

J‍M Driscoll

BOOK TWO: THE CHICAGO SERIES

Jennifer
DRISCOLL

This is a work of fiction. Names, characters, and places are the sole product of the author's imagination. Any resemblance to actual persons, living or dead, is entirely coincidental.
All rights reserved.

Copyright © 2017 by Jennifer Driscoll
Cover Design: BookBaby

ISBN: 978-1-54392-060-4 (Print)
ISBN: 978-1-54392-061-1 (eBook)

For Jake and Erin,
My biggest little fans…

And for my breast cancer sisterhood,
This book was too long in the making, halted by disease, overcome by loving support from a group no one ever wants to join.
Inspiration and love…

I've learned that home isn't a place,

it's a feeling.

Cecelia Ahern

Hailey Powers left Chicago at nineteen, vowing to never look back even if it meant leaving CJ Montgomery, and a piece of her heart, behind. She has changed in her time away – grown stronger, done things no one could have predicted, and raised a daughter almost entirely on her own. When she returns to Chicago under the most difficult of circumstances, she will be thrust into CJ's life and career, the very things he's made without her. She'll need his help and his heart. Can she go home? And when she does, will it be to a place or to a person?

CJ Montgomery has made peace with her leaving, at least that is what he tells himself to get through his days and nights. Thirteen years have passed since Hailey walked away – hand in hand with CJ's best friend, Jamie, no less. Are thirteen years long enough for a heart to forget? He's tried to let her go, made a life as a surgeon, a brother, a son. He's dated more than his share of women – more than his brothers' shares too. But there will be only one Hailey in his life, and he has always believed in second chances. When she reappears in his life, in his hospital, and in need of his help, will the choices Hailey made in life keep them reliving the past or give them a second chance at the future?

Powers' Pulse is a story of friendship, secrets, and letting love lead you home – no matter where or who that might be. Love finds a way.

Prologue

CJ held her hand… finally. Prior to that momentous breakthrough, the closest physical contact had been when he'd rubbed his elbow against hers during the James Bond movie they'd gone to see together three weeks prior. As Sean Connery had raced across the Venetian waters in his speedboat, Hailey's heart had accelerated, not at the scene in the movie, but in response to the glancing touch from CJ. At fifteen, that might as well have been a marriage proposal. She'd worked out the future of their relationship in her hormonal, adolescent head right up to the number of kids they would have and what they would have for dinner every night.

But when he held her hand, that was the real deal. He had invited her over for Men's Night at the Montgomery estate. The Montgomery men had given her an exemption, a free pass to join their evening because she was CJ's friend, one of his closest, and a constant at the Montgomery home. In her mind, the invitation plopped her squarely in the friend zone… no closer to CJ than his best friend, Jamie.

She would not learn until years later that the exemption was a sign. It was a signal from CJ to his two brothers and father that she was special. At sixteen, he was incapable of the grand gesture she'd seen in so many movies. This invitation was his gesture – to his family, to Jamie, to her... He wanted her close and maybe even fantasized in his own hormonal teenage mind that she was the one. If that was the case, the message to her, unfortunately, was lost in translation, in awkward immature signals and lack of communication.

She had arrived at the house wide-eyed and hopeful. Normally, she would just push through the large black door to her second home, but Men's Night seemed to call for more formality. After ringing the bell, she fidgeted, zipping and unzipping her jacket while waiting. Again, she rang. Again, she nervously fixed the collar on her shirt and smoothed the front of her jacket. Finally, CJ, winded from roughhousing with his older brother Kerry, pulled open the door mid-laugh. And then he did it. He reached out – unthinking, she was sure – and grabbed her hand.

"Hi." She was sure she was smiling like a kid on Christmas morning as she walked inside. *Chill out, girlfriend.* She let out a breath and relaxed her cheeks.

"'Bout time you showed up, Hailey. Now we can eat!" Kerry yelled from the other side of the living room.

"Ignore him. He's grumpy because Angela Darlington broke up with him. You look great, by the way. Just making sure you know it's pizza and *Star Wars* with my brothers, right?"

Damn it. She'd overdressed. She had tried on at least ten outfits before settling on this one. "I know. But I've never been invited to Men's Night before. I thought it an occasion."

"An occasion for Baby Drew to whine about the movie pick and Kerry to whine about… well, everything. Let me take your coat." CJ brushed a hand over her shoulder as he removed the light jacket, sending goosebumps down her arm.

The doorbell interrupted.

"I got it."

Swinging open the door, CJ stepped forward and gave his best friend, Jamie Powers, a handshake and a tug inside. "Great, now everyone is here. Let's eat." She deflated as CJ walked toward the rest of the men, leaving her in the overly grand foyer. Hailey recognized that her moment was over. He'd held her hand and noticed her clothes. Despite the brevity, she would hold on to the fantasy for a long time to come.

Jamie caught Hailey's eye, gave a warm smile and a nod of hello. "Should we go in or are we having pizza in the foyer?"

He wrapped his muscled arm around Hailey's shoulder and led her into the living room. She rested her head into his chest, trying not to sag.

Jamie touched her all the time. It was part of his personality to be a hugger, and at over six feet already, he had a habit of resting his hands on her shoulders from behind. She never thought twice about his physical interactions, never had the surge of pleasure from them the way any small touch from CJ raced over her skin. It would be a few more years before Jamie made any move toward an intimacy with his touch. But it would come, and she would fall for that openness, that honest affection.

With CJ, it would always be zinging thoughts and skipped beats. With Jamie, it would always be safety and strength. In the end, her choice was made for her. But she would always hold a place in her heart for glancing touches, spreading goosebumps, and James Bond.

Chapter 1

Chicago, sixteen years later

"You don't think this was an accident? That's what you're telling me right now?" Hailey fell into the chair next to Jamie's bed and took a deep breath of the dry hospital air. As if the shock of her husband's injuries weren't enough, this revelation sent her over the first hill of a roller coaster, that big one where you can't see the bottom until it's hurtling toward you at sixty miles per hour. The wind whirled by her ears, and her stomach rose into her throat. She squeaked the words past her breakfast. "I don't understand."

"No, ma'am. I can see that. Perhaps you should put your head between your knees and just breathe for a minute. You look very pale."

He'd moved closer sometime when she'd been falling down the hill, and he pressed a hand to her shoulder to nudge her forward. "Breathe, ma'am."

"Please stop calling me ma'am. My name is Hailey." Her voice echoed between her knees.

Kyle Collinsworth had been full of surprises since he'd walked into the ICU. His casual dress in jeans and an open-collared button-down shirt suggested friend. His calm grey eyes suggested sympathizer. But his FBI special agent badge suggested business – and questions.

"I know this is a shock, ma... Hailey. Probably an understatement for the whole situation. But having done this for a while now, I also know we need to keep it quiet on the chance that the person responsible remains close." Kyle sat next to Hailey without reaching out to her. They didn't know each other that well.

He had been a member of Jamie's first platoon, the one that had gone to Afghanistan, she thought. Or had it been it Iraq? It was hard to keep track this far out. Jamie had been abroad to so many different places.

"Listen. Did Jamie say anything unusual in the last few weeks?"

She lifted her head, noted the slight spin of the earth, and pressed her feet firmer into the floor. "No. Um... I haven't spoken to him for at least three weeks. Why? I don't understand."

"Did he send you anything... unusual? Unexpected?" Kyle persisted.

"Like what?"

Kyle turned closer and lowered his voice. "Anything on paper, voicemail that didn't make sense, gifts out of his character?"

"No, he didn't send anything unusual. Nothing comes to mind." She searched the unresponsive face of the man lying in the bed. She knew answers lay there, but there wouldn't be any questioning him now.

"Jamie came to me about six months ago. Said he thought he had discovered something at Wallace Security. Wondered if I could look into it."

"And did you? What did you find?" Hailey found herself getting defensive even though she had no reason.

"I tried. He tried. I asked a few questions but couldn't get enough information to file for any warrants. Jamie checked in with me pretty regularly. We'd meet for dinner or an early coffee. But then Jamie went off the radar. I couldn't get back to him before… well, this happened. What I know is that my friend Jamie, the Marine, the athlete, the father… he wouldn't have been careless with his steps or with his life. That's why I don't think this fall was an accident."

"So, what do we do now?" Hailey reached up to hold Jamie's limp hand.

"I'm just asking you to look for anything out of routine. Keep your head about you and let me know if anything seems off. I'll do what I can from my end. I don't have enough to open any kind of formal investigation." He reached into his shirt pocket and pulled out a business card. He wrote his cell number on the back and handed it to Hailey. "That's my personal cell. Call me if you come across anything."

She watched him walk out of the room, his long strides carrying him away from this sadness, her sadness. She wished that she could do the same, but her roller coaster ride was not nearly over.

Hailey traced the sunlight pattern on the walls as it moved through the white lace curtains, flowing gently in what there was of a late summer breeze. The diversion was a welcome alternative to the realities of the day. She lay in the king-sized bed filled with endless pillows and the soft feather duvet, but found no comfort, no sweetness. She knew it was because her husband lay across the city, in a stiff hospital bed, with tubes and lines running to the machines currently keeping his body alive.

She couldn't shake the eeriness of that first time walking into the sterile glass room in the VA ICU. It had marked an abrupt change in thinking. She had thought about it the entire flight north from Carolina. She'd barely been able to think of anything else. *What will he look like? What will have changed in his physical appearance?* She had neglected to anticipate the change in his *being*. Lying there, motionless, Jamie was no longer present. His body remained the same, but there was no soul, no life force, and she'd known it from the moment she'd slid the glass door closed that first day.

Today, seven days into his ordeal, her parents would arrive with Natalie in tow. How would she explain to their four-year-old daughter that her dad was no longer when she couldn't believe it herself? Natalie would see his physical body, but would she understand his loss? Would she know that he would be gone forever? They would be facing this world together as mother and daughter rather than as a family.

She disentangled herself from the bed, lead weights pulling her down, and made her way toward the bathroom in the hopes that a hot shower would wash away her thoughts – and her reality.

The curtains billowed again, bringing back thoughts of her own childhood here in the shadow of the big lake. She had grown up in an affluent suburb near the waters of Lake Michigan. She'd grown up in an intact family alongside her sister, Amy, complete with family dog and summer picnics. Truth be told, she had grown up in this Montgomery house. She had learned more here than at school. Here, under the watchful eye of Andrea Montgomery.

She stepped under the steaming, fragrant water and was lost in her thoughts. She'd fallen in love with two teenagers in these halls: Andrea's son CJ and his best friend, Jamie Powers. She loved them both in different ways. One in depth of friendship and one in depth of passion.

After leaving Chicago with Jamie, she'd kept up with Andrea by mail, email, and phone. When Jamie had had his accident, Andrea had been the first to call, not out of obligation, but from a place of concern, medical knowledge, and understanding of what was to come. Hailey had accepted the offer to stay at the family home without hesitation, as much out of gratitude as out of sheer denial that she would need to stay somewhere and for a good length of time. She couldn't stay with her sister, who was living in a one-bedroom apartment while she finished her master's degree in social work at the University of Chicago. She wouldn't have expected Amy to finish school living in such cramped space, especially after Natalie arrived.

And for how long?

No, it was a great gift to have the offer from Andrea to stay at the Montgomery family's home. She'd just have to be aware of CJ, keep her old feelings at arm's length, save her heart.

She stood under the stream, paralyzed it seemed, thinking of their childhood within these halls. They'd attended the same elementary, middle, and high schools. The three of them, Hailey, CJ, and Jamie, had been inseparable. They'd spent afternoons in CJ's loft room doing homework, listening to music, planning their weekends and their lives.

CJ'd had no trouble with homework. He was smarter than she and Jamie by leaps and bounds. It was intimidating how quickly he grasped a concept and became the natural teacher of others. He'd never made them feel as if they were less, just played off his ease by being the smart-ass or the comedian. He'd rarely gotten into much trouble, but he had never made things easy on Andrea or his father, JP. No one had really taken him seriously. Not even Hailey. She'd loved him in friendship, affection, admiration… and other ways that she didn't admit to even herself anymore.

She began to shampoo her riotous curls and rinse away the regret. When she almost couldn't breathe from the steam, she finally emerged to wipe away condensation from the mirror. Wrapping a towel around herself, she examined her reflection there. The dreamy teenager was gone, replaced by creases and worry, dark circles and fears. She thought of the days when her biggest worry might have been which bikini to wear at the beach or which movie they would see on Friday night.

She thought of Jamie.

He had been the consummate athlete. At six feet four inches, he'd towered over most other high school athletes. He had loved the attention of others for his physical attributes, his tremendous coordination, or his technical skill on a playing field. Academics had come second, often helped by CJ's tutoring.

She rubbed scented cream over her skin and tried to recall their best times. As their teenage years had hit, Jamie had been the first to show interest in Hailey's thoughts, her dreams, and her body. He'd been her first in almost everything… her first kiss, her first boyfriend, her first sexual experience – awkward as it was, and usually is, for two teenagers without a clue except an unyielding need to be somebody's something, their everything. She thought he would be her last, but the Fates had different ideas on that.

Slowly, she put on yesterday's t-shirt and jeans. She tried in vain to tame her wildly curling hair into a rough ponytail. And she thought.

They'd left town after high school. No longer Hailey Wilks and Jamie Powers, they'd been Mr. and Mrs. James Powers, headed for Camp Lejeune, North Carolina, and a military life. She remembered vividly his admission that he had joined the Marine Corps against the advice of his father. He'd been seeking her approval, her acceptance of the life he would make for them. It had been in the same conversation that he'd proposed marriage.

Jamie had become a Marine at a time when terrorism was a rallying cry for war and rebuilding the destruction of the very core of a country was expected of its victors. He'd spent ten years in and out of tours, rebuilding war-torn Iraq, scavenging the hillsides of Afghanistan, and in places unknown, doing the unknown as the unknown. He'd received little recognition stateside, nor had he wanted it.

Hailey was sure he had been most comfortable and felt most useful under the camouflage of night doing the deeds no American citizen would ever know had been done. He'd thrived there. He'd suffered on his return, with an aching to return to that team of anonymous men stamping out evil in the only world that made sense to him. He was not traumatized there. He was useful there.

Hailey had tried leading a normal life in the States while he'd been away. She'd finished school, earning a degree in computer science and early childhood education. She'd made choices for her own future. She'd met friends, gone to see movies, written letters to her husband… every day making choices that would change their lives. When he'd returned, she'd wanted to be useful too, but she could honestly say she had been traumatized. Their world had been. She had been alone so long she thought she could never be part of a pair again.

War and separation had changed them.

So had Natalie's arrival.

Jamie had tried living a normal life in their small Carolina home. Hailey had thought she'd made some improvements while he'd been gone – new curtains in the kitchen, fresh sage paint in the tiny bathroom, a small garden off the kitchen side of the house with basil and rosemary.

Jamie had questioned her choices. "When did we get this new silverware? How come the paper towels aren't under the sink?" Silly things to worry over, but everything seemed off-kilter, not quite straight.

Their physical relationship had been subject to the same angst. Jamie was a physical person. They had always connected that way. He used his body to show her love. She recalled sliding in next to him in bed several days after he'd returned, body and soul naked and anxious. Her body was different after Natalie and they hadn't been together in so long. He'd responded to her touch with a start. Nothing had been comfortable. They hadn't been able to find a rhythm, their rhythm. On a sigh, he'd rolled onto his back. All she'd been able to say was, "I'm sorry." She'd known it wasn't enough.

He'd gone out with friends, but he'd never invited her to join them. He'd needed his "guys' nights" to find that comfort that they no longer carried. The ease they had shared since childhood was gone. Their partnership was another casualty of war, of distance, of absence. She missed her husband every day of his deployment and every day since he'd returned.

Resigned to her current situation, she headed downstairs to seek out Andrea. She found Ms. Anna, looking exactly the same as she had all those years ago, serving pancakes and eggs to JP and Andrea at the small kitchen nook table. Andrea stood as she entered.

"Good morning, Hailey. How are you today? Did you sleep?"

Hailey hugged Andrea before nodding at JP over his morning paper and sliding into the booth seat across the table. "I'm okay. Natalie and my parents are arriving later today. Are you sure it's no trouble if Natalie and I stay? I know you work with children, Andrea, but living with a four-year-old, even temporarily, is a different matter."

"She'll be wonderful. She takes after you, dear. I've been trying to get my boys to bring me grandchildren for years. Besides, JP has always had a way with the ladies." She smiled at her husband, who raised his eyebrows as he peeked over the morning paper. "We have plenty of space. I'm sorry your parents didn't want to stay."

Hailey took miniature bites of her breakfast, attempting to cover her lack of appetite and spare Ms. Anna's feelings. "They'll be comfortable in their hotel. They have so many friends in the area. I doubt they will even spend much time there. They didn't want to be a burden."

"None of you are a burden. The situation is not the way we wanted to see you again, but we'll cherish the time we get together while you're here. It's been so long. I'm sure CJ will want to see you when he returns from his trip. He and Pete went to the Bahamas for a little R and R. He should have gotten in last night though."

Shifting in her seat at the turn of conversation to seeing CJ, Hailey changed the subject back to practical matters. "I'll be at the hospital most of the day, but I should be back in time to meet my parents and Natalie at the airport. Thank you for the use of the car and for the home… and, really, for everything you've done for Jamie and me over the years."

Andrea dismissed the gratitude with a wave. "Ms. Anna has a big dinner planned for tonight to welcome Natalie. Please invite your parents if they don't already have plans. Drew and Jillian will be here, and so will Kerry. Okay, I've got to make rounds. Love you both." Andrea bent over to kiss her husband's cheek and blew a kiss toward Hailey before leaving them alone.

JP put down his paper gently. "Is there anything you need, dear? I'm not the one to ask about the medical ins and outs – my wife and son are going to be your best bets there – but I can offer to help with any legal issues you might have to sort out."

"Thank you, sir. I'm not sure yet what they even are. Jamie's parents have been in and out, but I don't think they grasp the severity of his injury or the chance of recovery. They want to do everything in the medical system's power to maintain his body, which is what we're doing so far. They just haven't gotten to the idea that his brain, his soul, just aren't there in that room. I'm going to give them more time, but Jamie would not have wanted to live in the body he has now. Even if his brain functioned, the fall from that roof took his body and its power. He wouldn't want to live inside it in the state it's in. The next few days, or months, or even years are not likely to change that fact."

"Well, when it comes time to make decisions, we'll support you… and Jamie."

"Thank you, sir. I'd better get going."

"Sure, dear. See you and your Natalie for dinner tonight."

Chapter 2

"Ah, the smell of government-issued cleanser, fresh blood, and resident surgeon fear on a Monday morning. Good to be back at the VA, Jason." CJ smiled and shook his chief resident's hand in greeting.

"Dr. CJ Montgomery, nice to have you back. Hope you had a good vacation."

"Yeah, great. It was hot." CJ grinned and raised his eyebrows slightly. "The weather was good too."

An older nurse stepped between them and pushed her index finger into CJ's chest. "Like I taught you on your first day as a resident not so many years ago… Don't be an asshole!"

"Ouch. Maria, my love, you wound me." *Emotionally and physically*, he thought, rubbing his chest. He laughed it off as she moved on with her day in the ICU.

Jason gestured to the group of residents waiting nearby. "We're ready for rounds when you are."

CJ surveyed the crowd of young surgeons and students. "How are the new interns working out?"

"They'll do." Jason was momentarily distracted as his line of sight followed a set of tiny green scrubs into the nurse's station. A smile crossed his lips.

CJ chuckled and clapped his hands together in an attempt to gain the group's attention. "Good morning, team. Let's get started. Who's up first?"

Like a king holding court, he scanned the young, eager faces, eventually focusing on the shy brunette in the middle of the pack. He pointed to her clipboard and smiled. "Dr. Allen, who is your first patient?"

"Um, room 432. He's a thirty-two..."

Cutting her off before she could begin her presentation, CJ shook his head. "No, no. In the room, Dr. Allen. We present in front of the patient and any family members that may be present. Much more efficient." CJ placed his hand on the small of her back and gently nudged her toward the hospital room.

"Yes, sir," Dr. Allen murmured more to herself than anyone else, as the congregation of surgeons had already hurried into the room, where they surrounded the patient's bed and appeared to dwarf the already petite young woman sitting next to it.

On a nod from CJ, Dr. Allen began again. "Thirty-two-year-old male with a C2 fracture after a fall from approximately thirty feet, spinal cord injury on chronic vent support and G-tube supplement, day seven of hospitalization. Still unresponsive after removal of conscious sedation. No brain activity noted on EEG done two days ago. Status post splenectomy after traumatic rupture. Healing right orbital fracture, not thought to be a result of the fall injury. Pelvic fractures expected to heal without surgery. He is due for repeat CT of the brain today to assess swelling and then tracheostomy placement soon if the family has made up their mind regarding his ongoing care."

The last sentence came out with more annoyance than was intended by the young Dr. Allen. CJ dressed her down briefly with a short stare that she appeared to receive with the appropriate guilt.

"His family is right here, if you care to include me in his 'ongoing care,'" a woman's voice chimed in from the back of the group, her metal chair screeching as it moved back over the tile floor.

As she stood, her eyes met CJ's. The sharp sea blue had his memory suddenly shoot to nights on the football field, leather car seats, and the smell of movie popcorn.

"Hailey?" The air left his lungs with the admission. In a whisper, he dismissed all sets of eyes in the room, save one. "Everyone out. I'll meet you in room 436 in five."

The young surgeons looked from one to the other in confusion, without moving.

Shouting now, "I said room 436. Now!"

The team scurried out without a word.

CJ held her gaze until they were alone. "Hailey Wilks?" She was as exquisite as the memories that beckoned. And there were so many memories of Hailey.

She stood before him with her petite frame and gentle curves, her auburn hair curled around the elegant features of her face, including startlingly clear blue eyes that had the unique ability to look right past his exterior and into his inner thoughts. Today, those eyes were marred by the dark circles that had formed from worry and lack of sleep.

"It's Hailey Powers now, remember." She gestured and pulled away from his stare to take in the sight of her fading husband lying in the too-large hospital bed. "Jamie's smaller every day of the last seven I've entered this godforsaken room to sit by his bedside and wait."

"Jamie? Oh, God! Hailey, they didn't give me his name." CJ took in the body of the man who used to be his best friend, now minus the bigger-than-life personality.

"No, I'm sure not. Just the necessary stats of the day – recent vitals, overnight events, brain activity, latest EEG…" The mention of the EEG came out on a sigh.

"I'm sorry, Hailey."

"Did they give you his other stats?" Walking closer to the bed, she grasped Jamie's limp hand in her own. "Thirty-two-year-old man married at nineteen to one Hailey Anne Wilks, father of one adorable little girl, Marine veteran with ten years in combat service across the world? Those details seem to be lost in the heart rates, potassium levels, and ventilator settings. Hell, I'm lost in this glass box of a room."

"I'm so sorry, Hailey."

"I know, I know… Me too. I don't mean to snap at you." She huffed out a breath and sat back down in the metal chair. "It's been a long morning. And I hate this chair." Running her hands through her hair, she looked toward CJ and gave a weak smile.

He moved toward the bed, wary as the solidity of his medical world and the fragility of his personal life had just crashed into one another with the slide of the ICU door. "I can get another surgeon to attend, Hailey. If it's uncomfortable. If you don't want me… I know it's complicated."

"Of course I want you. You may be the only person who can help me here." She paused before going on. "I know I have to decide what to do for him, but it's… well, in your words, it's complicated. Jamie and I have been… separated for the last year. We have a young daughter and escalating medical bills. His parents want to keep going, keep up the treatments. I'm the one who has to decide what's best, and it's more than complicated."

"I'll try to help." Warily, he moved toward her, holding an uncharacteristically unsteady hand out to help her stand. "Come here." He pulled her into a gentle embrace and tried to soothe her nerves while every one of his own went on high alert. *Danger!* His head was shouting it from the rooftop, but his heart heard none of it, just the beating of a rhythm that had always been home, a rhythm that had faded but never extinguished, that had hurt and never healed – Hai-ley, Hai-ley, Hai-ley.

He pulled back, holding her at arm's length. "I've got to go finish rounds with my team. I'll come back when I'm done. We can talk through Jamie's medical issues. My mom will want to come see you. I know you two have kept up over the years."

Clearing her throat, she answered, "Yes, she knows I'm here. She's actually letting me stay at the house. I did miss her." Hailey sighed and tried to smile. "I'll be here when you're done. I've got to pick up Natalie and my parents at the airport by four. Jamie's parents are coming in again tomorrow from Florida. My job has given me some time off, but I've got a classroom to open up for the year…"

Tipping up her chin, he stopped her. "Hailey, slow down. I'll be back before noon. We'll talk it through." He turned to leave, his long strides carrying him away from danger, but he stopped short at the call of his name.

"CJ? I'm glad you're here."

A short nod of his head was all he could give without a complete betrayal of his feelings. He quietly slid the ICU door closed without looking back through the glass.

"Dr. Montgomery? Should we start back in 442? Your biggest fan with diverticulitis status post colectomy. She came off the vent while you were away, and the infectious disease team has cleared her to go with home care and IV antibiotics for the next two weeks. Should I discharge her without you seeing her today?"

"What? Um, no, I'll be right there." CJ took two deep breaths and slowed his pulse.

He and Jason rejoined the now buzzing gaggle of residents and students. They entered room 442 to find Mrs. Johnston sitting in the lone chair, dressed in her muumuu for traveling home today. This one, he noticed, had bright pink flowers clashing on a sea of blue, reminiscent of his recent vacation and not the worst of patterns he'd seen her wear over the weeks he'd taken care of her. He still had a hard time picturing a youthful Janice Johnston in the service, but she had apparently been a field nurse and earned several commendations in her time.

Her smile intensified as CJ moved closer to examine her. "Dr. Montgomery, don't you look tan and handsome from your trip? I healed up pretty good while you were gone." Her face fell. "Aren't you happy to see me today? Your eyes are sad."

Mrs. Johnston never stopped talking, not when she had ten out of ten abdominal pain, not when she had a fever of one hundred and three degrees, not until the moment the anesthesiologist put the mask over her face and chemically induced her silence. To his amusement, she had flirted with him throughout the verbal barrage, and to his dismay, she was occasionally far too insightful – one of those people with emotional intelligence to spare – and gave him a touch of the paranormal mind-reading vibe.

In his head, he had nominated Mr. Johnston for sainthood more than once.

"Always happy to see you, Mrs. Johnston. I understand you're ready to go home. Are you in any pain?"

"No pain today. My heart is breaking a little." She leaned in close to his ear as he examined her incision. She whispered, "As yours appears to be, son."

He glanced up at her kind eyes and found unexpected empathy from this unexpected source.

Pulling back, she addressed the room of surgeons. "I'll miss you all here. You've done a great job taking care of me."

"I'd say you're ready to get on home. The home nursing service will meet you there to continue your treatment."

"Is it wrong to have hoped you were coming home to take care of me?" A sly smile creased her chubby face.

"As much as I'd like to, administration frowns upon fraternizing with the patients." Giving her hand a squeeze, he gave her a sincere smile. "Try to stay out of my ICU, Mrs. Johnston."

"No promises, Dr. Montgomery."

CJ finished his rounds before he returned to Jamie's room. Hailey wasn't there. Relieved to be alone, he examined the body of the man he'd known most of his life but whom he'd lost long before this accident. Facial bruising, lacerations, soft tissue swelling – they all marred the face of the boy he'd called his best friend for more than ten years.

"What were you doing on that roof? Why weren't you with your family, your wife? Who had you become Jamie?" He sat near the bed, struggling to get past the bitter taste in his mouth, to think of Jamie in better times. They had grown up together, the three of them. Even as a child, he'd known better than to think that things wouldn't change, that *they* wouldn't change. He was a smart guy. He just hadn't expected it to hurt so badly when it hadn't worked out in his favor – when he'd lost her, them, his childhood all in the span of one day in August. He'd grieved in his own way, turned inward. He had dated women, probably more than his share, enjoyed many of them, rebuilt his confidence, but he had never forgotten his losses.

Gripping the loose hand of his former friend, he grieved the loss again. "Goodbye, my friend. I've missed you."

Hailey sat in the hospital cafeteria, scrolling through her phone. She knew CJ was behind her before he spoke – the air changed and a vague discomfort crept up into her chest. She felt his hand rest on her shoulder.

With a gentle squeeze, he asked, "Can I get you a coffee?"

"Sure, black would be great, hazelnut if they have it. I was just checking on Natalie's flight."

"Be right back."

She watched him walk away and smile at the barista, who gave him her best megawatt smile in return, and she felt jealousy. Not for the flirtation – God knew women had flirted with CJ his entire life. No, she felt a pang for the carefree nature of the smile. She was so tired of being alone. She was tired of being the responsible one. Everything had fallen to her – the house, paying the bills, finding the right daycare, making life decisions for a man she had barely seen in the last year. She was tired of breathing in fear and breathing out responsibility. There were no megawatt smiles in her life, perhaps with the exception of Natalie's. And even Natalie seemed to be catching on to her mom's ruse.

Hailey couldn't help but take in his features as he moved back toward her table. His tall frame and gentle touch gave him an elegance she had not seen in him as an awkward teenager. Those same mossy-green eyes captured her, as they had then. He wore his sandy-blond hair longer than most, brushed back off his handsome face with a little shaggy curl at the neck. His body had filled out, with muscular forearms, and she noted the hint of a bicep sliding out of his short-sleeved scrub shirt. She knew he wouldn't have lacked for female companionship, and she chided herself for the little bit of jealousy she felt at that thought.

Setting the coffee down in front of her, he apologized. "Hope that's doesn't hurt going down. They're not known for their coffee here."

"It's fine... That's all I can seem to say anymore. It's fine. I'm fine. We're fine. No one's fine, CJ."

Sitting down carefully in the chair across from her, concern sullied his handsome face. "I have so many questions. I'm not sure where to start or if I can even ask."

"It's okay to ask."

"Hailey, how did Jamie end up here? What happened with you two?"

She stared into the coffee cup, hoping the courage to be honest was somewhere in the reflection. "Jamie became a Marine. That is the only thing I can put my finger on. I know I changed too over the years, but really, Jamie came back a different man. He'd gone to Iraq, Afghanistan, who knows where else. He looked forward to going back." She waved her hand in the air as she spoke, as if she could touch those places or push them aside.

CJ appeared to stare through her, out the windows of the hospital, and into the distance. "I know I can't ever fully understand that. To look toward war?" He returned his stare directly at her. "But to look past you and your daughter?"

"I don't think he intended to in the beginning. Jamie came home from abroad. He had a knee injury while in Iraq. He was reluctant to report it because he knew the consequences. It went as he expected. He was thanked for his years of service, sworn to secrecy on the missions he'd participated in or known about, and he was discharged honorably. As you might imagine, he was destroyed."

She drank a small sip of the hot coffee, not tasting it, and went on. "I wasn't enough for him. We barely knew each other after so many years apart. He tried living a normal life in our small Carolina home. Everything seemed off-kilter, not quite straight, you know? Even our baby girl wasn't enough. No job was fulfilling. He missed his team and his work. This last group, Wallace Security, he seemed to find a place there. It's based here in Chicago." She hesitated, unsure how to phrase her next thought. "I didn't want to leave my job or pull Natalie out of her school. Honestly, I wasn't sure it would stick. So… we stayed, and he left."

CJ whispered back, surprised. "He left you?"

"It wasn't like that. We didn't really talk about it as a separation, but that's what it was. I didn't want to come back to Chicago. To follow him again…"

CJ shifted in his chair. "I'm sorry. We can talk about something else. We should talk about the plan for his care. What do you understand to be his prognosis?"

She let out a nervous laugh. It was involuntary. Confusion spread across his brow. "I'm sorry, CJ. I didn't mean to laugh. It's the irony. Don't you see? CJ, the serious surgeon with the serious face. I just never could take you seriously."

"Well, we've all changed, Hailey. You may not take me seriously, but I do. I perform surgery on human beings. I save lives. I cure illness – every day. I have a serious job, and right now, I need to help you make some real decisions." Anger and hurt leapt into his voice.

"I said I'm sorry. I know Jamie's not up there in that glass room. His body is there, but Jamie isn't."

"Why does he have an orbital fracture? It wasn't from his fall."

"I don't know. I told you I hadn't seen him in months. I'm not sure what he's been doing." She practically yelled it across the small table before reining in her temper.

"Was this really an accident? Do you know anything about the firm he was working for?"

She shook her head. "Not much. He only told me that they do security for companies moving inventory in and out of the city. Mostly art, I think. He joked about escorting some beautiful women around."

"If you don't mind, I'll ask my dad or Kerry about the group. Just to see what kind of place it is. Okay? Now, when do Jamie's parents get in?"

"Tomorrow. They were here right after the accident. They had to go back to Florida to settle the house and plan to come back up for a longer stay. They think he'll be in rehab by the time they get back. They have no idea how broken he is."

"I'll make sure it's clear. I'll help them understand. But… you know that you have all the rights here." He cleared his throat before going on. "You, as his wife, can make the decision to continue care or to stop. I know you'll find it very difficult, but I would advise you to consider stopping. He could be an organ donor. He could save more lives. He'll never live the one he wants again."

"I know that… I do. I need to spend some time with my daughter and my parents. We'll make a decision soon."

CJ's phone beeped with a text message. He glanced at the phone and then leapt to his feet. "You may not get to. Jamie's coding."

They ran side by side to the bank of elevators and pushed to call the car. Three more nurses in scrubs joined them inside, notified by the same text of her husband's demise. Of course, they had no idea who they were running to. They ran because it was a life, a person, injury… pain.

She stepped out of the elevator, into an organized chaos, and tried to stay out of the way. CJ took the lead, directing other surgeons to begin CPR and nurses to give medications by the IV. She stood outside the glass door, gripped with fear, not even totally sure she wished for one outcome over another. She watched them bring her husband's body back to life. Nothing could bring back his soul.

Emerging from the room, CJ brought her chin up gently with his steady fingers. "He's back. He's in sinus rhythm, and his blood pressure is holding for now. Go get your daughter. Do what you need to do. I'll see you at the house later."

She stared into his moss-green eyes, tears at the verge, and recognized the boy he'd once been and the man Charles Montgomery had become.

Chapter 3

"Mommy!" Natalie ran off the escalator and into her mother's arms – her precocious four-year-old with masses of curling brown hair just like her own in childhood. She had Jamie's dark brown eyes and a button nose. She was outrageous but sweet, tough but vulnerable, too smart and wise beyond her years.

"Oh, sweet girl! Mommy missed you very much." Holding Natalie at arm's length, Hailey looked her up and down. "I think you've grown in the week since I last hugged you!"

"Grandma says you grow in your sleep. I've been sleeping good at Grandma's house, Mama. I'm big now."

"So big."

Natalie held out two fingers, sort of like a peace sign but tipped forward for her mother to touch with two of her own. They had dubbed it "Deuces," and it was her own unique way of saying, "I Love You."

"I love you too, baby."

Hailey grasped her little girl's hand and moved to hug her father and mother in turn.

"Hey, Dad, how was the flight?" Her father, Mason Wilks, had been a respected accountant in Chicago before retiring five years before to work on his golf game and manage a few rental properties they had acquired during previous visits to Florida. He appeared to have put on a few retirement pounds, but his skin was deeply tanned from recent time in the sun and good Mediterranean heritage.

Mason whispered in her ear as they hugged, "It was fine, love. Hug your mother. She's been a mess all week."

Her mom, Sandy, smiled weakly, the epitome of a Southern belle. She was petite, polished, and forever in love with her husband. Raised as a debutante in Georgia, she and Mason had met when he'd been finishing officer's training in the Navy. Sandy had learned in toddlerhood that her own appearance reflected on her family, and Hailey was not sure she had ever seen her mother with a strand of her platinum blonde hair out of place. She had been an executive secretary to her father after they'd married. She'd loved details then, but now worried over just about every detail of life.

Hugging her daughter, she started in. "We almost missed the plane. Your father ignored the GPS the entire way into the airport, and we hit construction traffic. Then the bridge was up for fifteen minutes…"

Mason shook his head with a chuckle. "We made it just fine. She even had time for a coffee at the airport. Miss Natalie had hot chocolate." Her father raised his eyebrows and nodded sideways toward Natalie as if to say, "How about that? She's still alive, and so am I."

"Thank you for bringing Natalie up. I'm not sure how long we'll be here. Things are not good at the hospital."

Her father took her other hand. "We'll stay as long as you need. Now, let's get our bags at the carousel."

Natalie's carousel Spidey-sense perked up. "There's a carousel at the airport? I want to ride the white horse."

"Sorry, baby. Not that kind of carousel. You'll have to ride on Grandpa instead." Sandy smiled. "He's always been my white knight. It's fitting he'd be hers."

***

Ms. Anna, the Montgomery family housekeeper of more than thirty years, swept a piece of lint off the corner of the dazzlingly white tablecloth in the formal dining room. The table was set for eight with fine china and sparkling silver.

"Oh, Ms. Anna! You've done too much. I thought we were having a simple family dinner?" Hailey ran her hand over a pretty plate and napkin.

"It's dinner for a princess. Is Princess Natalie coming down? She's my right-hand girl in the kitchen after today. She and I have some dessert to finish."

"Yes, she'll be down in a minute. She was accessorizing." Hailey smiled and rolled her eyes at the thought of her young daughter dressed to the nines for the family dinner with a family that wasn't even her own. Hailey had spoken of the Montgomery family so many times that Natalie probably thought of them as royalty. The dinner table, and Ms. Anna's special treatment, were not likely to dissuade her of those thoughts.

Kerry, the oldest of the Montgomery sons, entered the dining room quietly. His tall frame fit the grandeur of the room, but his gentle nature had always betrayed the exterior. He smiled at Ms. Anna and took Hailey into a warm embrace. "How are you, Little Mama?"

She buried herself in his chest. "Oh, Kerry. It's so good to see you. Will I ever live down that nickname?"

"You always took care of us boys when we were kids, like a miniature version of my mom. Now you are a mom. Don't think the nickname is going anywhere. Your daughter is a beauty. Takes after Little Mama."

"Why is it that some woman hasn't stolen your heart yet, Kerry Montgomery?"

"Ahhh, ever the matchmaker. Who's to say someone hasn't? It's all in the timing, my friend."

She laughed with Kerry's strong arms wrapped around her and peered up into his grass-green eyes. She slapped his chest in mock protest. "You're holding out on me."

"I'll let you know when she knows." He gave her a wink and let go to greet Drew and a gorgeous blonde who could only be his new wife, Jillian.

"Sorry we're late… Hailey! Come here, Little Mama." Drew, CJ's younger brother, punched Kerry in the arm when he winked again at Hailey, noting the nickname. Then he drew Hailey into a comforting hug. Stepping back, he made introductions. "This is my lovely wife, Jillian. Jilly, this is Hailey Wilks… Powers. Sorry, Hailey."

"Very nice to meet you, Jillian, and congratulations on your marriage. Baby Drew here was always my closet favorite for tying the knot first. It's good to be right every once in awhile. Ah… and here is *my* favorite girl." Picking up her daughter, who'd come into the room running at full speed dressed in a miniature ballgown, tiara, and bangle bracelets halfway up her arm, she turned to introduce the Montgomery brothers. "This is Kerry, Drew, and his beautiful wife, Jillian."

Natalie gave high fives to both men and giggled. "Hello, boys!"

Jillian laughed. "Oh, you are in for it, Hailey. There's a mischievous teenager in there."

Laughing, Hailey set Natalie in her seat. "That or the next president of the world."

JP and Andrea entered the dining room together, holding hands – a sight so familiar to the family that no one even noticed any more. Hailey did. They were a pair, a team, partners. She reflected on her own partnership – broken, lonely, missing. She was not sure she would ever have what the Montgomery parents had, or even anything close. She was going to be a single mother, a teacher, a daughter, but she wasn't sure she had it in her to be a wife or partner to anyone again.

It was impossible when you only felt like half a person to give half of yourself to someone else.

Just as dinner was being brought to the table, CJ walked in, and her thoughts flew out. He was as handsome as she'd ever remembered, now out of his scrubs and wearing a tailored suit, crisp white shirt, and silvery-green tie that matched his eyes almost exactly. He bent over to kiss his mother's cheek and whispered, "Sorry I'm late. I had a meeting. I did bring a present though." As he stood, a tall blond man with light-blue eyes and a strong jaw line walked in behind him.

Smiling, CJ introduced his guest. "I brought Scottie for dinner."

"Scott, so nice you could join us. Ms. Anna, we'll need one more place setting, please." Andrea rose and began to move chairs herself to accommodate their family friend.

"Hailey, this is Scott Cannon. He's worked with JP for years, since college. Right, Scott?" Andrea made quick introductions. Hailey gathered that Scott was dedicated to the shipbuilding business, mostly the paper-pushing side, and rarely left the office, let alone joined the family for dinner. He greeted JP and Kerry with a handshake each before settling next to Hailey for the meal.

Hailey spoke quietly to Natalie in the seat next to her. She pointed at CJ and whispered in her daughter's ear. They both laughed before Natalie spoke up.

"CJ, you are the prince. Sit by me! Sit by me!" She gave him her full megawatt smile, the Heart Melter.

"Well, this is awkward. If I'm your prince, I should know who you are."

"I'm Princess Natalie of North Carolina, silly goose." She made everyone at the table laugh.

CJ played it up, very seriously saying, "Of course you are. I'd be honored to sit next to you, Princess." He nodded to a smiling Hailey before taking his seat. "You keep on laughing there, Little Mama. If you'll recall, this prince has a tower."

"Oh!" Hailey felt her heart break just a little at the thought of that tower, three floors up in the Montgomery house with views of the lake and memories so long forgotten of fanciful wishes and stolen kisses. "I remember." She caught his eye and knowing smile as the first course was served.

Conversation varied among the small groups at the table. Hailey learned that Drew and Jillian had married on the Fourth of July this year, a surprise to everyone but Andrea and Jillian's father. Drew was running a small boat-building business locally and doing quite well. Jillian worked as a barista in a fun little local coffee shop and, if Hailey had heard correctly, played drums with a band occasionally. Hailey liked her immediately, and Drew looked so happy.

She remembered Drew's friend Molly, who was apparently Jillian's half-sister through a rather convoluted story filled with intrigue and ending with Jillian in the hospital. Molly now had a son, Sam, who was close to Natalie's age and might be a good playmate while they were visiting.

JP and Scott mostly talked business with Kerry. She was shocked to hear that pirates remained a plague to the industry, especially along the African coast. She'd thought they had disappeared into her history books.

"Scott, that's an interesting tattoo on your hand. Do you belong to a pirate crew? What does it mean?"

Scott looked down and frowned at the Roman numeral II on his left hand. "It means I was a stupid teenager once. I grew up in a rough part of Chicago. Didn't always make the best decisions." He seemed to be lost in thought for a moment.

Hailey answered as if in confession with the priest. "I was a stupid teenager once too."

Kerry smiled. "If you were a stupid teenager, then the rest of us never had a chance. I never got a tattoo, but I recall CJ and I breaking a few bones in a car crash on our way back from that college party we'd snuck into. That was the end of any thoughts I had of following in Mom's footsteps."

JP shook his head. "I don't think I've ever been so mad at you two boys. But CJ fell in love with surgery that night. And his nurse. Good thing for Princess Natalie only the surgery part stuck."

The table laughed as Hailey looked over toward her daughter. She leaned down to pick up Natalie's napkin from the floor, only then realizing that Natalie was holding CJ's hand under the table. Her heartbeat accelerated. A call from Andrea at the head of the table brought back her wayward thoughts.

"Hailey, where are your parents this evening?"

"They are out visiting the Wilsons in Schaumburg before they check in at the hotel. My dad will likely talk Dennis into some golf while he's here. He thinks he has skills now that he is retired and has a putting green in his back yard. I'll meet them at the hospital tomorrow."

The room fell silent at the word "hospital." Hailey realized the subject had been avoided through the entire evening, clearly on her behalf. She let her eyes fall onto her gold wedding band still present on her left hand.

"Speaking of the hospital, I think one of my patients tried to hit on me today," CJ said playfully, breaking the silence with his usual comedic grace.

Natalie turned with a frown. "But you are my prince, CJ."

"Of course, you are right, Princess Natalie, but I think Mrs. J might have something to say on that subject. She has something to say on just about every subject." CJ rolled his eyes and laughed.

Natalie nodded her head in affirmation. "She and I will have to have a talk."

"I guess you will." He smiled over at Hailey, who tried to convey her embarrassment over her daughter's precocity.

Dinner concluded with a lovely Michigan cherry pie that had the flakiest crust Hailey had ever tasted. Natalie took full credit while Ms. Anna just smiled along. As the dinner dishes were cleared, Natalie's eyelids began to droop.

"It's been a long day. This little princess needs her bed. I'll take her up. Thank you, Andrea, Mr. Montgomery, and Ms. Anna for a wonderful meal."

"Let me take her, Hailey. It's been so long since I tucked anyone in." Andrea's gaze moved slowly from son to son, conveying the appropriate level of guilt to each for not providing grandchildren to date.

Kerry chimed in, saying, "Save us, Hailey. Give her the child. Let her have her fill."

"Are you sure? She's like a sack of potatoes when she is out."

"I can handle this thirty-pound sack of sweetness." Andrea lifted Natalie out of her mother's arms as Hailey gave her one more peck on the forehead. "Go catch up with the boys. I'll stay up there in case she wakes up. JP and Scott have retired to the office. There's brandy or wine in the game room if you want anything. I'll see you in the morning. Sleep well."

"Thank you, Andrea."

Hailey turned to join the younger crowd in the living room and was transported back to her teenage years. She had spent so many evenings lying on those couches, dreaming of faraway places, planning a life with children and a home of her own. Back in the here and now, she saw three Montgomery men, no longer boys, now in business suits or with labored hands. They served as their own evidence that they had all grown up to face life's challenges. It was nice, she thought, that they had each other even if they didn't always appreciate it.

CJ laughed at something Drew said and then turned his head as she entered. Smiling and relaxed, he rose gracefully from the couch. His shirtsleeves now rolled to the elbow, he held out an elegant hand to Hailey. "Let's go for a walk out by the water."

"Sure. I don't want to go too far in case Nat needs me."

"Princess Natalie will be fine with the queen. And we're not going far."

The hot, humid August night was like walking into a wall. The lake had gone quiet, with virtually no breeze on the night air. Hailey felt the pressure soak into her bones, rising as they walked in silence, without touching, toward the boathouse.

CJ cleared his throat. "I spoke to Scott today about Wallace Security. I found him in the Montgomery offices after I finished at the hospital. That's why he came back to the house with me. He says they run a good company and they've helped Montgomery Shipping with several transit details recently. He hadn't met Jamie, but he says everyone involved has been professional. Thought you might like to know."

"Thanks, CJ. It helps. I can't imagine Jamie working for any other kind of company." The summer moon sparkled off the nearby lake. "I missed it." She nodded toward the lake for CJ's reference. "I missed your family. And I missed you."

She stared out at the lake, knowing she wasn't yet ready to look him in the eye. Not until she had said her piece.

"I know you're waiting for an explanation… for why we left. I keep thinking, will it be enough? Would anything?"

"Try me." CJ bent down to pick some grass at his feet. He fiddled with it in his fingers, betraying his nerves.

"We were teenagers. We thought we were in love. Jamie had a riotous personality, larger than life, of which, you are well aware. I wanted to live that life with him. I wanted to be needed by him, by anybody, really. That didn't last very long. Ironically, as it turns out, I've lived alone for most of my adult years, at least before Nat arrived." She peered down at the grass tickling her bare feet. "You didn't need me as much. You didn't really need me at all, CJ."

"I didn't need you as much?" he whispered more to himself than her as he appeared to process what she was saying. "Let me get this straight. You left with Jamie because he needed you, and you thought I didn't?"

"You were off in college, as you should have been. And Jamie and I, well…"

"You and Jamie what? Just spit it out, Hailey." He threw the shredded grass in his hands down to the ground.

Here goes, she thought. "I was pregnant."

"What?" CJ turned back toward Hailey. "How? But Natalie…? I don't understand."

"You're a doctor, CJ. You know how this works."

"I get that. But… you never told me."

"I didn't tell anyone. We didn't tell anyone. My parents don't know to this day. I… I lost the baby after we got to North Carolina. After we were married." She debated internally how much to share, but she'd come this far. She'd swim down a little further before coming up for air. "I lost my heart when I lost the baby… I became a different person after that. It's not all Jamie's fault that things fell apart for us. I only just started to feel whole again when Natalie was born. I was so scared through her pregnancy, alone, unsure if I had done something to lose the first, unsure if I would get to see her small hands, her happy eyes."

He sat roughly onto the bench swing near the water and pushed his fingers through his hair. Hailey watched the moonlight glance off the highlights, illuminating what had been lost so many years ago.

Frustration warred with love. "It's hard to hear," he said, "and I'm sorry that you had to go through that. That you weren't happy. That you were alone. I always thought of you. I hoped, if nothing else, you would be happy." He stared out at the lake as if he'd been there a thousand nights, whispering a thousand prayers. "Always."

Hailey came to his side, sat quietly, folded her arms across her chest, and rested her head against his shoulder. "It all seems so long ago now. That baby, that life… it was everything then. It's not that I didn't love Jamie. I did. But that baby was reason enough to leave my family, to get married, to leave you. But we didn't do it well. We were just teenagers pretending to be adults. I pretended a lot back then. I told myself that you were where you needed to be. That I wasn't in love with two men. One, too much a fantasy. One, very much too real. Most of the time, I tell myself it just wasn't meant to be." Pressure filled her chest, her heart laid bare after all this time, waiting for his reaction, his inevitable anger, but it never came.

"I always wondered, selfishly, if I meant to you what you did to me, but I was too proud to ask, and then you were married to my best friend. Now I guess I know. And for the record, I needed you as much as anyone. It was no fantasy, Hailey. I was afraid of a lot back then. Afraid to let anyone down. Afraid to tell you how I felt." He smiled for the first time. "Thankfully, I'm not the same guy anymore. I've built a life here. Done things no one thought I could."

"I saw that today. We have all changed. I'm not the same person I was then. You don't know what I've done in my life. You don't really know who I am now."

"The thing is, I think I'll always know you, Hailey." He sighed and then raised an arm around her small shoulders, kissed her temple, and rested his head against hers. "My pride was wounded, but my heart has always been here. Waiting. Did you ever think of me, Hailey?"

She couldn't help but whisper back with honesty, "Always."

Chapter 4

"But his heart is beating! Why would we stop treating our son?"

Hailey cringed inwardly at Paulette's use of the word "we." It was part of her mother-in-law's personality to accept credit for others' accomplishments. Hailey recognized that. Paulette had done it so many times when Jamie had been in the service. Now she was taking credit for the work of the doctors and nurses keeping Jamie alive.

She and Randy had been in Florida most of the week before arriving early that morning. They hadn't sat through days of surgeons' rounds, IV changes, procedures, and bad news. Hailey would not begrudge their intimacy as Jamie's parents, but she did take issue with their implied proximity. The last time they'd been in the same room as their son, Jamie had just returned from his last tour and Natalie had just been an infant. They were blissfully unaware, as far as Hailey knew, of their son's marital discord or internal struggles.

"He won't ever walk again. He won't talk again. He's not in there, Paulette. His EEG is flat. His brain is not swollen. It just doesn't work anymore. It's not going to work anymore. His body won't last much longer. CJ says he could be an organ donor. He wanted that.

We had talked about it." Hailey sat back in the wooden chair slowly to let the words sink in.

"But his heart is still beating! He can stay on the machine and be alive." Tears crept up over the frustration in Paulette's world. "He is our son! We should be able to decide."

CJ leaned forward over the small table centered between Hailey, Paulette, Randy, Jason, and himself. He spoke quietly, efficiently. "Actually, this is Hailey's decision as Jamie's wife. She has the legal authority here."

"I don't want to upset anyone, especially you, Paulette. But Jamie would not have wanted this life." Hailey sighed and considered her wedding band. "He was so full of life. He was proud of his skills, his physical attributes. He was a man who worked with his body, played sports with his body… He loved with his body." She looked shyly up at CJ, who didn't flinch at the words. "He would want us to stop trying to fix what can't be fixed. He's gone."

Randy stood and walked toward the small window in the conference room. He stared out through the hazy view at the city below and was obviously lost in thought.

"Randy, we cannot let this happen. We can take this to court if we need to. We can take care of him. I'm not giving up on my son. Our beautiful, brave, strong son." Paulette turned with tears in her eyes to stare at her husband.

Without turning away from the window, Randy calmly asked, "Can we have some time alone, please?"

"Of course. We'll be in his room if you need us. We have to change a central line. That should take about twenty minutes." Jason stood and turned to CJ. "I'll go set us up."

"Thanks, Jason. I'll be right with you."

CJ and Hailey turned to leave together. Once in the hallway, Hailey bent forward, hands over her knees, and began to cry. Awareness of the nurses and therapists in the ICU was the only obvious thing that kept CJ from pulling Hailey straight into his arms and never letting go.

"I haven't cried. Not in this whole mess. I told myself I'd cry when it was over. At first, I thought that would be when he walked out of this hospital. That was before I got here and saw him. Even then, when his body was there but his presence was gone, I didn't cry. I thought about what I would tell Natalie. How I had to be strong for her. But do you know what happened? I brought her in there this morning, and she didn't even flinch. I told her, 'Daddy is sick. He's here in the bed.' And she said, 'No, he's not here. He was in my dream last night.' Even she knows he's not in that room."

Taking a deep breath to steady herself, she went on. "I kept thinking, what if that was Natalie. While Paulette was talking in there, pleading for her son. What if that was my child in the bed? Could I give up? I'm sorry, CJ. Like I said, I haven't cried."

"Hailey, you have every right to cry, but you have to know that you're doing the right thing. They'll come around. We just need to give them a little more time."

"Okay." Pushing herself up to stand and pulling herself together, she wiped the tears from her eyes. "I'm fine."

He took a step closer and lowered his voice to avoid the ears of his coworkers and friends. "No, you're not. I'm not. There is nothing about this that is fucking fine. It's tragic. Horrible. It's the end of a man's life. It's you, and it's me, and it's Jamie." With a sigh, he ran a gentle hand over her hair. "I have to go do my job. Let me know if you make any decisions."

She nodded roughly and sniffled back her tears without looking up. The world seemed a little smaller as he walked away.

⌒✦⌒

CJ couldn't hit the bag any harder. He would if he could. As a surgeon, boxing was not the preferred form of exercise even if it was just sparring or bag work. Your hands are your livelihood as a surgeon. They should always be protected. It sure as hell felt good though.

He'd returned to his loft apartment, which he had always loved. It was modern in space and size, but with warm touches in the exposed beams and interior brick walls. He'd bought it just out of residency as a present to himself. Drew had made several pieces of furniture for him, including a huge dining table centered on the largest window, just off the kitchen. He'd filled the rest of the space with comfortable chairs, a leather sectional couch, and a few pieces of modern art he had been drawn to. The loft was within walking distance of the two hospitals he worked out of most often. Other friends and his two brothers were close. When needed, he could be at his parents' home in under ten minutes. The fact that Ms. Anna dropped in often to clean and leave him a home-cooked meal didn't hurt his heart either.

The long bag hanging in the far corner had called to him when he'd come home. Despite the emotional fatigue of the last few days, it felt good to use his body. To be honest, it felt good that he *could* use his body. With each punch, he had a physical reminder of his own strength. He couldn't help but think of how his friend had lost so much.

He reflected on his conversation with Hailey by the lake. He was floored by the idea that he had lost her because of a lack of need. When he was sixteen, he hadn't thought that he needed a single person more than Hailey Wilks. She was the start and end of his days. He'd failed to see the connection between her and Jamie because he hadn't wanted to. In those last weeks at home, he'd wrapped himself up in getting ready for college. He had hoped to return the conquering hero. He'd never thought he'd been competing for Hailey's heart against an actual hero. It had never even occurred to him that he would lose – until he had.

They had come to see him at school, just before his sophomore year. They'd been dating the entire year he'd been away, but neither had let on to any change in the relationship. When they'd come to visit, he'd recognized the change in their intimacy immediately. They'd stood a little closer or sought the other's approval a little too much. Hailey hadn't even been able to look him in the eye. When they'd walked away from his dorm room, hand in hand, he'd gone to the gym then too – to work off the energy and work out his thoughts. He had come so far, and yet, here he was, back in between the woman of his dreams and his best friend, punching a bag that couldn't break, unlike his heart.

He had managed to work up a pretty good sweat by the time his brother Drew knocked on his door.

"Hey, come on in."

"Hey. You look like shit. Aren't you coming to the game with us tonight?" Drew wandered into the kitchen and pulled out a bottle of water from the refrigerator for each of them.

CJ wiped sweat from his eyes and shook his head. "Thanks. Love you too, little brother. I don't think so."

"Sam will be disappointed. He was hoping fun Uncle CJ would catch him another fly ball."

"The one I caught last time was lucky enough. Lucky too, the kid didn't fall off the upper deck reaching for it himself." CJ downed the bottle in one long pull before walking back toward the punching bag and his therapy session.

Drew followed him across the apartment. "Princess Natalie will be disappointed too. She and Sam hung out together today and, I hear, made all sorts of plans for eating their way through the baseball game."

"Is Hailey going?" CJ stopped punching and realized he was short of breath at the answer rather than his workout.

"No, she and her parents are meeting some friends, but Natalie has convinced her to let the princess come with us. She has never been to a professional game. And for a girl of four, she knows an awful lot about baseball."

"Mason loves baseball. Her grandpa has to be the one who taught her. Hailey certainly never took an interest."

"You don't think it was Jamie?" Drew was clearly treading lightly at the mention of Jamie's name.

"No, from what Hailey told me, he didn't actually spend too much time with Natalie. He hadn't seen her in the last year. He was here, and they were in North Carolina." CJ started lightly moving around the bag, working on control rather than velocity. "Can you believe that? He left them in North Carolina. And he was here, in the city, for a year." He hit with more power.

"He didn't bother to look me up once?" Hit.

"Stop by for a beer?" Hit.

"Or a punch in the face?" Hit.

"CJ, you're his doctor right now, for as long as he has. She's his wife. Stay out of that." Drew was now holding the long bag for CJ to aim. He peeked around. "Is something already going on?"

"Baby brother, it's been going on since I was nine." He threw one last solid punch and changed his mind. "I'm gonna jump in the shower. Looks like my princess and I are going to a baseball game."

Natalie was adorable in her pink Tigers baseball cap with sparkling fake diamond studs at the points of the Old English D. She was so excited when Drew and CJ showed up at the house to take her along.

"I didn't know the Tigers were changing their colors to pink and white, Princess Natalie," said CJ.

"They're not, silly boy. Grandpa gave it to me. It's for the girl Tigers. Are we gonna catch a fly ball? Sam said you know how to do that."

"We'll see what we can do." He rubbed a hand over her cap.

They headed off together – Drew, Sam, CJ, and Natalie. The strange part to CJ was that it didn't feel odd at all. It felt natural to hold Natalie's hand crossing the street or lift her up onto his shoulders as they climbed the steps to their seats. She didn't seem fazed by it either.

The only part where he might have regretted their lack of adult female companionship was the first trip to the men's restroom with Natalie dancing along beside him. There were a lot of questions he didn't know how to answer about urinals and lack of stall doors. The lack of cleanliness didn't seem to bother her as much as the general male negligence in leaving it such a mess. But they made it through, and the second and third trips were easier.

Without exception, he had never seen a boy eat so much food in his life as Sam, who packed it away during the game. He must have set a new personal best for hot dogs eaten, slushies drank, and peanuts shelled. It was adorable how Sam played host to Natalie, explaining between bites that the family was rooting for the Tigers mostly and that the game was important tonight, as the season was coming to an end and the Sox were a division rival. Natalie nodded along with due reverence, and Sam appeared to be pleased with himself.

"Why do you like the Tigers, CJ? They don't belong to Chicago."

"Well, Princess, when my brothers and I were about your age, we went to a baseball game exactly like this. My grandfather took us."

"Grandpas are good. They know lots of things and stuff."

"Yeah, they're the best. Well, my grandpa was a big Tigers fan. He put me on his shoulders, taught me how to keep score, and taught me how to root for my team. After a while, he taught me how to throw a ball and hit homeruns too. Do you want to play baseball?" He could only hope she didn't say she wanted to be a cheerleader or a ballerina, things he knew nothing about.

"No, I want to be the coach." She beamed, the Heart Changer. "Will you teach me?"

"I promise." And there it was. He had fallen. His heart was swelling with the promise of some kind of future with Natalie. He would support Hailey in her choices. But if she chose to leave, he was quickly realizing that it was going to be harder than it had been in college to let her walk away.

Hours later, CJ carried an unconscious Natalie into the guest room at his parents' home. He tucked her into the overly large bed and kissed her sweet forehead before turning on the princess nightlight.

"Thank you, my prince." She smiled gently, rolled over, and was gone again into sweet, sleepy oblivion.

CJ tiptoed out and all but closed the door, careful not to make too much noise. He exhaled and leaned back against the wall, exhausted and thankful for its strength.

"Hey, I'm glad you're back. Looks like a successful outing, Dr. Montgomery."

CJ rolled his head, still resting against the wall, to see Hailey standing there in a long silk robe, pulling the sash just a little tighter at the sight of him. She took his breath away. She was a woman, no longer a girl. She was a mother, not just in nickname but in reality. He found himself wanting to pull her into an embrace, to run his hands through her hair, over her shoulders, and down the sides of her waist. To ease her worry and his own. He wanted to release that belt, release the woman beneath. But she wasn't his. And neither was the girl sleeping in the room behind him.

"I always think it's a successful trip if she falls asleep on the way home. You did good, CJ."

"I didn't catch a fly ball for her, but she seemed to have a good time anyway. She certainly ate enough to sustain herself for the next few weeks."

"If only kids were bears hibernating in the woods. Then that would be true. She'll be pulling on Ms. Anna's apron by morning. Thank you, CJ, for taking her to the game and taking her mind off her dad."

He pushed himself away from the wall and stood directly in front of her, taking in the evening light off her skin, savoring the quiet privacy of the night. She smelled of lilacs and sweet powder. He found it, and her, intoxicating. "I enjoyed it myself. She's wonderful, Hailey. You've done well by her. How was your night?"

"Not as distracting, I'm afraid. I had dinner with my parents and some old family friends. I got a call from Jason at the hospital that Jamie's blood pressure was falling intermittently and they had to add another medication to keep it up. I told them not to call you unless it was an emergency."

She looked down at her toes, painted pink little more than a week ago, when life was so much easier. "I've made my decision. I know what I need to do. I just don't think Jamie's parents are ready to hear it. Will you help me, CJ?"

He pulled her forward, into his arms, as he'd wanted to do in the hospital just hours earlier when the tears had finally come. He hadn't been able to allow it in front of his coworkers then, but here, in the quiet of his family's home, he could do as he wished. He wanted to keep her there, safe in his arms. He bent forward and kissed the top of her head. "Always."

Chapter 5

Hailey sat quietly at Jamie's bedside in the metal chair she despised and held her sister's hand. Amy hadn't been able to get away from her exams and the clinical work for her internship at the Children's Hospital next door. Until today, she had seen Jamie only once since the accident, and it had been immediately after Hailey had called. Then it had been chaos with emergency surgery, test after test, and treatment options. Things had changed dramatically since that initial call. Amy hadn't seen him lying helpless in his gown. She hadn't seen him shrinking slowly from the world.

"He wouldn't have wanted this." Amy wiped the tear from her eye with her bare hand. She wasn't usually one to cry. Hailey's little sister had been tough as nails growing up. Where Hailey had been the little mother to the neighborhood kids, Amy had been the father figure. She'd bossed everyone around, big or small, and taken no crap from any of them. It was a trait that Hailey often thought would make her a good social worker. She was fiercely loyal to Hailey and had seemed to understand almost immediately when Hailey had confided in her over a year ago about the change in her relationship with Jamie.

"No, he would never have stood for this. He's tried to die several times since getting to this place. We just haven't let him…"

"Did you talk to… his doctors about the possibility of organ donation?" Amy stood to hold Jamie's hand and brush the hair from his forehead.

"You can say his name, Amy. CJ is his doctor. He's working on it."

"How are you doing with this? It has to be impossibly hard to be here, next to Jamie day after day, making choices for him when you two hadn't been together for so long. And to have CJ be involved?"

"CJ's been wonderful, to me and to Natalie. His whole family has been gracious and kind. I'd forgotten. I was so far away, by myself and then with Natalie. I'd forgotten how much I need Mom and Dad, Andrea Montgomery, you. I've been closed off to everyone but Nat for too long. It's been good to be back, despite the circumstances. I have so many memories of the Montgomery house, the Montgomery boys… and CJ. It helps to remember how Jamie was then, so alive. It makes it a little easier to know what to do for him now."

"You never talked about him… about CJ, I mean. Since you went to North Carolina, I hadn't heard you even say his name once."

"Just thinking his name was too hard for a while. Then, well, I closed that part of my heart – the part I kept for CJ. I was a dedicated wife and then a mother. I loved Jamie when he was the boy I knew and the man I married. It was wonderful to love him then. It all changed slowly, so slowly I didn't even realize it was happening. I closed that part of my heart too – the part I kept for Jamie." With a sigh, she closed her eyes. "I'm just now remembering how wonderful it was to love them, both of them. But we're not teenagers anymore. People change. We've all grown up. We live with the choices we make."

"Do you regret going to North Carolina? Do you regret marrying Jamie?" Amy came to sit with Hailey again, to resume the vigil.

"No, not regret. I can't regret loving Jamie or having Natalie. She's my world now. I'll do anything to keep her safe and happy."

As CJ stepped in front of the glass door to room 432, she had to quickly put aside what that might be. His tall frame was covered in dark-blue scrubs, and a surgical mask dangled around his slim neck. His badge read "Dr. Charles Montgomery." Hailey couldn't help but think it belonged to someone else. She pictured some old man with white hair who'd spent his life in an operating room or a lecture hall, not the joking, playful teenager she'd left on a dorm doorstep so many years ago. The man in front of her now was capable, strong, and loyal.

"Everything is all set up." Turning toward her sister, he opened his arms wide. "Amy, it's been so long." CJ wrapped her in a quick hug before returning to the job at hand. "We've got the transplant teams on standby. They'll plan to harvest Jamie's heart and lungs for a single donation destined for a cystic fibrosis patient in Houston. His kidneys are going to patients in Washington state and California. His liver has a match in Detroit. He'll save at least four lives today… I can see a little doubt in your eyes. You're doing the right thing, Hailey."

"It's not doubt. I'm just not used to the medical stuff like you two are. Harvest? Is that really the word they use? These teams of doctors and nurses?"

"I'm sorry if it seems a little cold. You forget in medicine that everyone else doesn't talk like this. The teams are preparing now. Are you ready to do this?"

"Yes, it's time. Jason said he wouldn't make it much longer. His blood pressure is falling again. Jamie's parents are here. I'd like to give them the last moments with him but… I need a minute to say goodbye."

"Do you want me to stay, Hailey?" Amy squeezed her hand.

"No, I need to do this alone. Thank you for coming this morning. I know you've got to go to your internship."

"Forget about that! I'd do anything for you. You know that, right?" As Amy gripped her shoulders, Hailey gave a quick nod, still staring down at the floor.

Amy moved over to the bedside and grasped Jamie's hand. "Goodbye, Jamie." She leaned down and kissed his forehead one last time before moving slowly out of the room.

"I'll give you some time." CJ nodded toward the bed.

"Thank you, CJ. For everything." Hailey pulled the metal chair close to the bed and sat at her husband's side while CJ moved quietly from the room.

She fussed with his gown sleeve and straightened the IV line at his side; she knew she was stalling. The ventilator hissed in and out, keeping time or, now as she reflected, counting it down. "Jamie,

I don't know if you've heard me at all over these last few days. For my own sanity, I'm going to assume that you have."

She cleared her throat, hearing the steady beat of his pulse transmitted to the monitor hanging above, proving his heart's strength with each beep. "I have loved you as long as I can remember. Your life was my life. That's what we promised each other when we went to Carolina. I don't regret a moment of our time together. We grew in two different directions, but I have never regretted loving you. I will never regret having your beautiful daughter as a daily reminder of that love. She is the best part of both of us. I'll try to take good care of her, keep her safe as you always did, and teach her what a good man her father was." A tear fell from her cheek, landing on the gold wedding band still present on Jamie's left hand. "God, this is hard. Goodbye, my love, my husband, my friend… Jamie." She stood and slowly pressed her tear-stained lips to his cheek.

Outside the room, Paulette and Randy were wrapped together in an embrace, tears streaking down Paulette's cheeks. They stood as she closed the door for the last time. Unexpectedly, Randy pulled Hailey into his strong arms. She nodded silently and sobbed into his chest. After a time, she pulled back to look into his deep-brown eyes.

"We're going to sit with him until they take him to surgery. Do you want to stay with us?"

Shaking her head side to side without removing her gaze, she whispered. "No. I said my goodbye. I'm going to be with Natalie. I need to be with her."

She pulled away from Randy, away from her past and toward her future.

As she walked down the hall, in the distance, she could see CJ sitting alone in a row of chairs, hands in his hair, staring at the floor. As she stepped toward him, he raised his head. Tears clogged the corners of his eyes. She felt pulled to him, toward his pain, as it was her own. As she reached his chair, he stood, gathering her into an embrace so tight she thought she might not breathe again. She melted into his arms. Chest to chest, she could feel his racing pulse, in sync with her own. She knew he felt it too. His embrace tightened. The pain of it brought her back to the present. She wouldn't go numb in her grief. She would feel it, all of it. She would share it with CJ, with Natalie, with everyone who loved Jamie.

Chapter 6

Hailey tugged on the huge entrance of the downtown office building. She fought the wind to pull the unyielding door open a fraction of an inch. From behind, she felt a tall man reach above her hand and help move the monstrosity. Looking up, she stared into the light-blue eyes of Scott Cannon and watched the smile trace across his lips in triumph.

"I could have gotten it… eventually."

"I have all the confidence in the world that you would have, Hailey. It's nice to see you again."

"You're stronger than you look, Mr. Cannon. Thank you."

"Please call me Scott. What are you tunneling into the building for today?"

They were pushed close together and forward by the droves of others entering the building in a tidal wave – every soul talking or texting on a device in front of them while simultaneously pushing the wave forward, toward unseen progress.

Stepping to the side as she entered the granite-filled lobby, she answered Scott's curious stare. "This is where Wallace Security is based, right? I didn't realize Montgomery Shipping and the security firm were in the same building. I have to pick up a key to Jamie's apartment from reception. I've got to sort that out and pick up his uniform for the funeral."

"We could have sent a messenger to do that. Still can if it's too hard, Hailey." His features softened as he moved a windswept stray tress of hair from her forehead and tucked it behind her ear.

Slightly uncomfortable by the intimacy of the moment amidst the bustle of others coming and going, she took a step back. "Can you help me find reception?"

"The fair Katrina behind the far desk will be able to help you." He pointed two fingers toward a blonde-haired goddess sitting cross-legged in a brocade miniskirt and stiletto heels. Hailey didn't miss the rolling of his eyes as he placed his hand on the small of her back and moved her toward the Plexiglas desk. She was sure this woman had requested the stylish material just to expose others forced to wander past to her God-given genetic superiority.

"Katrina, this is Mrs. Powers. She is here to pick up the key to her husband's apartment in the State Street Building. Could you please find that for her now?"

"Of course, sir." Katrina's expression changed to one of compassion as she looked back to Hailey. She rose gracefully to procure the key from the mailroom located behind her desk.

"Thank you, Scott. You've been very helpful. I know you must be busy. I won't keep you any longer than I have." Feeling uncharacteristically sheepish, Hailey tucked the wayward strand of hair behind her ear again.

"My pleasure entirely. Good luck today. I'm not sure why that sounds like the wrong expression for what you have to do today." He pulled a sleek sheath from his jacket pocket and placed a Montgomery Shipping business card into her hand. "I'm very sorry about your husband, Hailey. My personal cell is on the back. Don't hesitate if you need anything else."

She watched Scott's tall frame move easily toward the private elevator and disappear into its walls. She thought she'd like to do the same when Katrina returned with the same weary expression she'd seen on just about everyone who knew Jamie had passed.

"Where did Mr. Cannon go?"

"He's gone to his office. Do you know him well?" Hailey wasn't entirely sure why she was asking.

"No. He's not an extrovert, that's for sure. Spends more time in this building than anyone else. Can't say that I've ever captured his attention. I did know Jamie a little. He and I would chat on occasion when he waited for Mr. Cannon in the lobby. He told me about your little girl. I'm sorry about his passing and your loss. He was always nice to me. I liked him very much." She handed the key to Hailey gently. "You know where the building is located?"

Feeling a bit less hostile toward perfect Katrina, Hailey answered, "I have the address. Thank you. I'm sure I can find it."

∞

Hailey picked up the package from the super before climbing the stairs to the second-floor apartment. She had called Jamie's platoon leader, Matt Callahan, two days prior to have him get the dress blues from their home in North Carolina. Jamie hadn't taken them on his move to Chicago. When she'd made her decision at the hospital, she had called Matt for the uniform. And now, here it was, heavy in her hands. A military funeral, the thing she had feared perhaps most while they were married, was now imminent.

She pushed the key into the lock of apartment 2B, allowed herself into the space, and set the package on the living room table. As she glanced around the studio apartment, she saw familiar items – some clothes she recognized as Jamie's, a small television he'd brought with him, some linens from their home in North Carolina. She saw things that were new – a video game system, a pile of yellow dishes in the sink, and a small pink jewelry box engraved with "Natalie" in script on the top.

Hailey picked up the box and ran her fingers over the grooves of the name. She lowered herself slowly onto the bed as she opened the lid. "Twinkle, Twinkle Little Star" floated out of the small speaker in the corner as she did so. Tears filled her eyes. They had not been forgotten… well, at least Natalie had been present in this place with Jamie. That was a comfort.

Inside, she found a small charm bracelet with princesses dangling from its chain and a key with a black flash drive attached by the keychain. She picked it up to examine it, noting only the number two written on one side of the drive. "An odd place to store your files,

Jamie. And where's number one?" She ran a hand over the felt-lined box but found nothing else inside. She placed the keychain in her pocket and began to look through his clothes for the necessary items, the ones she'd come for originally. She needed to find his cell phone. It hadn't been recovered at the time of the accident. It might be helpful to Kyle. She also wanted some more-personal items, including his cross necklace and, if not overwhelmingly abrupt to her olfactory sense, his lucky socks.

Jamie had not been known to be a neat freak, and that trait seemed to be just as evident living alone as it had been in their small Carolina home, perhaps worse. The necklace and the socks were easy enough to find. After thirty minutes of searching, she gave up on the cell phone. She suspected it had been lost during his accident, probably at the bottom of Lake Michigan. It was not in this mess Jamie had called home.

She pulled a box from the closet and began to load it with the uniform, the necklace, and the socks. Turning back to the bed, she placed the pink jewelry box on top. She already had a plan to come back to pack up the things she would bring back to Carolina and to donate the rest locally. She reflected back on the space. This was who Jamie had become – quiet, separate, unfamiliar.

Slowly, Hailey closed the door.

"Who's ready for a ride?" CJ smiled brighter than usual. Hailey saw it for what it was – an attempt to cheer, to distract, and mostly to empower Natalie.

"We can't wait! Right, Nat?" Her own voice seemed ultra-high-pitched, shrieking, just a little too excited.

"Mommy, I need my life chest!"

"Life vest, sweetheart. It's in the boathouse. Let's go find it." Without need of further encouragement, little summer jelly shoes skipped ahead on the path toward the boats.

"I guess we are going for a boat ride." Hailey shrugged and gestured for CJ to follow.

CJ put an arm around her shoulder. "It'll be a good distraction. Nothing more can be accomplished today. As hard as it will be, tomorrow will come either way." He gave her a kiss on the top of her head.

"She needs a distraction. And so do I, if I'm being honest."

They followed Natalie into the modern boathouse and toward the classic wood boat bobbing gently on the Lake Michigan waves.

"Is this your boat, CJ?" Natalie asked, jumping up and down in place.

"No, sweetheart. This belongs to my dad." Leaning in close to whisper in her ear, he clarified. "Really, it's Drew's boat, but he lets my dad think it's his."

"Parents!" She rolled her eyes and giggled with CJ. The sound was sweet, the sweetest.

Together, they gathered the needed life vests and untied the beautiful craft, launching into the sparkling lake waters and away from the sadness of dry land.

"You're sure you know how to drive this, right?"

"I got it. Don't you worry, ladies. Now, which end is the front?" Hailey laughed at his horrible attempt at a joke. It felt good to give into the feeling, to breathe a little easier.

Hailey plopped Nat onto her lap and stared out toward the horizon – sun just beginning its descent toward land, night just beginning to rise, a night in which she would not likely see much sleep or gather much rest.

"Go faster, CJ." Natalie's eyes were alight with the prospect.

"Yes, ma'am." CJ put the floor shift into forward and turned the throttle lever on the steering wheel. The boat whisked through the chop of Lake Michigan waves and out toward the orange horizon. Squeals of glee followed from both Hailey and Natalie. They raced against the coming day and against the past heartache.

A few swerving turns later, CJ slowed the boat to a crawl, and Nat hopped off to sit on her own in the last row of seats. Before long, the rocking of the waves had her asleep on the soft leather. Hailey covered her with a towel for protection from the late day sun and sat back down in her seat next to CJ.

"She's so sweet, Hailey. She's going to be fine tomorrow. How about you? You okay?"

"As good as I'm getting today." She changed the subject. "I missed this view."

"The other side is my good side… Oh, you mean the lake."

She giggled at another pathetic attempt at a joke but relaxed a little nonetheless. She patted the dash in front of her. "You should be proud of Drew. He builds a fine boat."

"I always have been. Just don't tell him that." He smiled down at her, blocking the sun, casting shadow over her seat.

"Next time I see him…" She thought of the funeral tomorrow. That would be the next time: when she buried her husband, the father of her child, her friend.

"Hey, hey. Don't go there. It won't help. Stay here with me, right here." He slid her over to rest her head on his shoulder and comfort them both. He rested his lips in her hair and whispered, "Right here with me."

Chapter 7

"My dress matches yours, Mama." Natalie sat primly on the back seat of the limousine, waiting for Thomas to take the driver's seat. She wore a black and white polka-dot dress with a full skirt and black patent leather shoes. "Thomas said I looked pretty. You look pretty too."

"Thanks, baby. Thomas will take us to the funeral for Daddy. Do you know what a funeral is?"

"Yes. Grandma Sandy told me we are going to say goodbye to Daddy. I'm wearing my princess bracelet that he got me. I love it." She tipped her two fingers forward in her sign for I love you and rested her head against Hailey's arm.

"Right, baby. Lots of people will be sad. Everyone loved Daddy. Will you help me be strong today? Be my big girl?"

"Okay. I am big, Mama. Will CJ come? I can hold his hand, and you can too. Then we'll be strong."

"Yes, love. I'm sure he'll come. Lots of Daddy's friends will come. The Montgomerys and even Ms. Anna. She knew Daddy too, when he was just a kid like you. And grandpas and grandmas will be there too, of course."

"Mama, will you sing my song on the way? The robin song?"

"Sure." Hailey put her arm around her only child and sang the song she'd sung while her baby had been in her womb, or sick with croup, or just overtired and cranky. The song was about a lonely little robin waiting for a mate to come home. It was Natalie's song and far too appropriate for the moment.

Thomas started the long, black limousine, and they made their way slowly to the cemetery. As they entered, she saw the casket, covered in the American flag, being pulled by a set of two large horses toward the site. Then she saw them.

All of them.

Jamie's platoon in full dress uniform in the scorching heat, waiting at the site, hands up in salute as the casket moved toward the rectangular hole made ready for the day. A tear fell down Hailey's cheek. They were all there. She hadn't asked. They hadn't called. But here they were, ready to salute their fallen brother and pay respects to his service and his family.

"Who's that, Mama?"

"They are your dad's brothers."

"Daddy had brothers?" Natalie scrunched her eyebrows together.

"No, not that kind of brother. These are the men he stayed with when he was away." She couldn't think how to describe these men she knew were so important to Jamie and so foreign to Natalie. How could she describe what they'd meant to him or how they were related? Not by genetics, but still by blood… and by war.

The limo pulled up next to the many stones that marked previous losses, and the door efficiently opened. Expecting Thomas to be there, Hailey reached out for some gentle assistance and found herself pulled into CJ's embrace.

"Anything you need today. Anything," he whispered in her ear as he released his hold.

"Thanks, CJ. Could you help Natalie walk over while I say hello to the men? I can't believe they're here."

"I hope it's okay that I called Matt." He peered down at her, searching for reassurance.

Hailey looked into CJ's eyes, her breath lost for an instant. "You called them?"

He tilted his head toward the men. "Go. I've got the princess."

"Thank you, CJ." Her hand slid down his expensive suit coat and past his hand that was just then reaching for Natalie. She placed thick black sunglasses over her raw eyes and dropped her stare to the ground, walking carefully toward the ceremony.

The flag-heavy casket sat on risers over the grave. Small folding chairs, reminiscent of the hospital version that still plagued her memory, lined either side. Most were already filled with family and friends, including Jamie's parents and her own. The Marines approached Hailey cautiously, with respect. Each leaned forward to give her a solid hug before returning to their line for the service. The pastor gave some brief remarks, of which Hailey heard about ten percent. She could hear Paulette softly weeping. She caught Randy giving quiet endearments in return. To save her broken soul, she focused on the stars of the flag, on the scent of lilacs in the air, on the memory of Jamie.

It was the gun salute that brought her back to reality. Hailey sat at the side of the casket to receive the flag. She'd seen the ritual before at the funerals of other men returned from war, but she'd never heard the words whispered in the passing of flag and shells.

One shell is for God.

One shell is for Country.

One shell is for the Corps.

On behalf of the President of the United States, the Commandant of the Marine Corps, and a grateful nation, please accept this flag as a symbol of our appreciation for your loved one's service to Country and Corps.

As "Taps" played, each note echoing off the ache inside, she helped Natalie toss a rose onto the casket. Tossed her own. And then it was done.

She felt warm arms encircle her, but she didn't know whose they were. She couldn't bear to look at each person, to see the hurt and the loss in their eyes. She never shed a tear until Thomas finally closed the door of the limousine. CJ slid into the seat next to her and held on. He wrapped an arm around her hunched shoulders, saying nothing, and gently nudged her against his body. She wept, truly wept, for the first and last time.

The arrangements were lovely. Andrea Montgomery had done everything she could to take charge of the nagging details of the reception and allow Hailey to grieve with her family and friends. She pushed through the black front door, as she had hundreds of times in her youth. The house was the same as it had always been, with a faint lingering smell of teakwood candles and chocolate chip cookies. It still offered warmth and care, even as it welcomed Jamie's family and friends for a gathering of grief and of stories. Some were funny, with the laughter increasing as time moved away from the sadness of the burial. Some were poignant. And some were blaringly untrue. But Hailey let them be told. They all needed to be told.

"I can't believe he's gone." Matt took the vacated seat next to her at the patio table as Hailey watched her daughter play soccer on the lawn in her bare feet and ballgown. "It seems like it would have been easier to believe if it had happened while we were overseas. There, it's a fact of being. Here, it's inconceivable."

"I know. And of course, I don't fully know. I'm glad you came today. All of you. What are you doing now, Matt?" She reached over to lay her hand on his. It twitched at the connection, so much like Jamie.

"I'm working mostly. I got out a little after Jamie. Took a job with Wallace just before he did. I travel mostly for them. I'm glad I was home when Dr. Montgomery called."

Hailey turned toward Matt. "Andrea or CJ?"

"CJ called. He told me about the arrangements. He wanted to make sure it was all done right, military, you know. He asked for my help, and I couldn't be anywhere else. I miss Jamie."

"Me too. I've missed him for a long time."

"Hailey, did he tell you what he was working on? Did he ever share any of it?"

"No. He and I talked about Nat mostly. He talked practicalities. Did I have enough for daycare? Did he need to send more home? He was so closed off at the end. He didn't need me anymore."

"Don't let yourself think that. He loved you."

"Not enough. We both knew that at the end. He'd stopped sharing his life with me when he moved back to Chicago, when he left us."

"Hailey, I'm sorry. I introduced him to the job. I'm sorry it hurt you. What will you do now? Head back to North Carolina?"

She squeezed his hand. "That seems to be the question of the hour. And I just don't know yet." Hailey watched her four-year-old daughter racing around the yard, her hands thrown up in the air, cheering Sam's goal. "I just don't know."

CJ closed the sliding office doors quietly and exhaled. He had sought out his dad's office because he knew it would be empty and the liquor cabinet full. He needed a drink and ten minutes of quiet. He hadn't expected his father to be at the desk.

"Well, handle it, Scott. For God sake, we don't need any press on this. Not after Wallace and the other incident last year. I'm counting on you to figure it out. I'm aware of the external players in this. Figure it out." JP set the phone back in its cradle firmly and took a sip of his brandy. He picked up his head to see CJ staring at him. "Jesus,

CJ. You scared me. Took a few years off me there. Do you need something, son?"

"I didn't think anyone was here. I was just looking for a quiet space to take a breather."

"I was doing the same. Want a brandy?" JP stood to move toward the decanter on the mahogany sideboard.

"Sure. What were you doing?" CJ sat quietly on the leather chair near the bookshelf, resting his elbows on his knees.

"I had a few phone calls to make."

"You can't put it aside for one day? This one day?" CJ snapped at his dad when he meant to take it out on himself. He'd been feeling pressure to get back to work but had been reluctant to share it with anyone, feeling obligated to help Hailey through her toughest time. He took the brandy snifter with a shake of his head.

"Not that I should have to explain, but we had an issue I needed to sort out. I've got a ship at sea on a return run for repairs that hasn't been heard from in several days. Scott's on it, but I was getting an update. I'm going to ignore your childish behavior for today."

"Yeah, I'm a child. Maybe one day, you'll see me as a man."

"I don't think this is about you and me right now. I'm sorry you're hurting, CJ, but don't blame this on me. I'm going to find your mother and help where I can. I suggest that you do the same." JP laid a hand on his son's shoulder before moving toward the door.

"I'm sorry, Dad. You're right. I don't blame you."

"I know, son. Finish out the day. Go help Hailey finish out the day."

"Yeah, I'll be right out." Sitting heavily back into the chair, he pushed down the brandy and felt the fire down his throat. His heart was heavy, pulled down with feelings of loss. *Right back where it all started*, he thought. No, he was a different man now. He would deal with this in a new way, speak up, take what he'd always wanted. He wouldn't hide himself this time. He could only hope he was enough, that he'd made himself into enough… for her.

∞

"Baby Drew. Have you seen your brother?" Hailey, now casually dressed in jeans and a sweatshirt after everyone but family had left the reception, wandered out of her room and caught Drew in the hall.

"Hey, Little Mama. Which one? I have two, one being more of a pain in the ass than the other."

Hailey shrugged softly as if resigned to her fate. "The bigger pain in the ass."

"I think he's in the game room. I'm headed there too. I believe my saintly wife may be with him." Drew took Hailey's hand gently and pulled her toward the room. He looked at her sweetly. "Are you going to be okay?"

"Nothing's for certain in this world, Drew. But I've got to think of Natalie and have a little hope for our future." With a shy smile, she stopped short and gazed upon the two they sought, asleep on the comfortable couch with an old black and white movie still playing on the TV. Jillian was resting her head on CJ's chest, where he had undone his tie and half the buttons on his dress shirt. They were exquisitely peaceful and utterly gorgeous in sleep.

"How can she take my breath away while she sleeps?" Drew looked fondly down at the pair.

"Because you know she loves you and you're not sure you can give as much back. There's a fear in love. I've always thought that was the spark. Like teetering on the edge of something. It takes your breath away, but in the best possible way. She looks exhausted though. Is she working too much, Drew? With the coffee shop and the band…"

"No. It's the baby. I hear growing one is hard work." An enormous grin split Drew's face as he peered down at a shocked Hailey.

"Oh, congratulations! It's so fast. Is she healed after her injury?"

"The doctor says yes. And we want a big family. She's always wanted a big family. I told her I'd do everything in my power to give her all that she wants. So, I made the ultimate sacrifice and…" Hailey was slapping his shoulder to make him stop his preening.

"You did good, Baby Drew. Does Andrea know yet? I can't believe she could keep that a secret. She's so ready for a grandchild."

"No, just you…and CJ. We're waiting a little longer to tell everyone. The family has been a little distracted, which is fine. It's all new to me, but I'm told we should wait awhile to tell everyone. Just to make sure everything goes smoothly. Right? You've done this."

"Yes, you're right. With Nat, I waited until we had the ultrasound before I told even my mom. I'm sorry to be the source of the distraction recently and the sadness at a time that should be so happy. I'm thrilled to keep your secret though." Hailey reached over to wrap her arms around Drew's chest in a congratulatory hug.

"What secret are you keeping?" A sleepy CJ adjusted his body without opening his eyes or waking Jillian.

"That you're leaving medicine to join the circus as the bearded woman."

"Oh, that. Hailey, could you put him in a headlock for me. I can't disturb his pregnant wife, who, you'll notice, is currently nuzzled up with her better-looking brother-in-law."

"Funny, I don't see Kerry." Hailey and Drew laughed together, which, unfortunately, woke Jillian from her sleep. Drew bent forward to press a kiss to her forehead and lift her from his brother's arms.

"I'm taking my bride to bed upstairs. While I can still lift her."

Jillian slapped his chest. "Don't make me hurt you, Andrew James Montgomery."

Drew turned back at the door to watch CJ smile and gently tug Hailey onto the couch, taking the warm spot now left vacant by his wife. "Secrets everywhere tonight," he whispered to an already-sleeping Jillian before pulling the door shut behind him.

"Did you get the princess to sleep?" CJ stroked Hailey's hair gently as she lay against his chest, soothing her shattered nerves and setting her skin tingling at the same time.

"Yes, she was out before I closed the door. It's been a long day… for everyone."

"And how are you holding up?" The lazy rhythm he set as his hand glided through her hair felt good. Too good. She missed that kind of touch, that gentle pet that could soothe away life... or death.

"I'm not gonna lie. I've had better days. I appreciate everything your family did today. Everything you did for me and for Natalie. She's so in love with you, CJ."

"The feeling is mutual." She felt his heartbeat accelerate. She heard it with her ear pressed against his chest. Her stomach twisted at the same time. She knew he couldn't leave things as they were. He needed to know where he stood. "How about her mama? Can her heart be won?"

"CJ... what can I say? It feels strange to think that way, on this day. I won't deny that my thoughts go there sometimes. But is it wrong?"

"Wrong to whom? It's just you and me, Hailey. Nobody else matters."

"Natalie matters. I have to think of her."

"I just told you that I'm in love with her. She's amazing, brilliant, special. Just because you've had her, you'll never think of yourself again? You'll never need love, partnership, friendship?"

"I want those things. Of course I do. I'm just not sure I'm capable of accepting them or giving them back to anyone. I know you think you know me, CJ, but I'm not the teenager who left here so many years ago."

"And I'm not that boy you left. I don't want to be that boy. I want to explore who we've become, who we could be. I've done enough waiting, Hailey." He pulled her chin up to look into his moss-green eyes. "I need you to catch up."

This kiss was not one of friendship or comfort, as it had been by the lake, not a casual peck on the temple or a gentle greeting on her cheek. No. This kiss drew on passion. It toyed with pain. Pain felt so long ago and for so long after.

His tongue teased her lips, coaxing them open to move more fully into her, into her world. Her heart jackhammered in her chest, too fast to slow down, too strong to be stopped.

"CJ."

"Don't. Don't think. For just a minute."

And she was under again. Not thinking. Feeling everything. He pressed his hard body to hers, requiring that she feel his realness – his reality. She couldn't deny the pressure. She wanted the release.

His lips moved from hers to seek the line of her jaw, up to her ear and down the side of her neck. Each touch required another. His hands ran circles over her back, pushing, guiding her toward him. She reached up to hold onto him and to the world now spinning with her. She grabbed that sandy-blond hair at the nape of his neck, felt its softness. Her fingers splayed on his cheek, felt that rough edge of unshaven jaw. Air escaped her lungs with every kiss.

He swallowed it up. He drew out more. And then… his heart may have stopped.

"Not here, CJ. I'm sorry. Not like this, on this day." With a tear on the verge of release, she stood and pulled away. He watched her walk toward the door, watched her try not to run for her escape. Before he could find the words, she was gone. He dropped to the couch, closed his eyes, and swore at himself for pushing too hard.

"CJ, there you are. I just saw Hailey heading up to her room. She's upset. Is everything okay?" Andrea sat quietly next to her second son and rested her hand on his rigid back.

"Would you believe me if I said it was?"

"No. I know my boys better than that. But I'll listen if that's what you need."

"I'm afraid of what I need. What I need just walked out. What I need lies sleeping next to a princess nightlight on the second floor."

"We don't always get what we need, CJ. Hailey knows that better than anyone right now. She's had a long day… a long two weeks if we're counting. If she wants what you're offering, what you are, then she'll find a way to it." She ran her hand over his back in soothing strokes. On a sigh, she whispered, "Love finds a way."

He sat back at that and ran his hands through his hair. "I've always thought so. When I was waiting for her, I always thought so. Now that she's here, now that I can touch her, how do I make sure she finds it?"

"You'll think of something. You've always been a smart boy."

It wasn't smart, but it sure as hell felt good. The hot amber liquid slid down with a burn that couldn't be ignored. It would eventually bring on the numbness that allowed him to ignore everything. He sat alone in the game room, Scotch whiskey bottle in hand, heavy crystal tumbler in the other, and sank into the couch cushions with disgust. He'd pushed her away. He'd pushed her too hard. She had buried her husband that day, and he'd pushed her further. What kind of a friend was he? What kind of a man was he? She didn't need him to save the day.

The day was a loss.

"You're not usually the insomniac. That's my calling." Kerry sat down carefully on the furthest couch cushion.

"It hasn't been a usual day."

"That's the understatement of the year. You want a beer instead?"

"No. This will do nicely. Thank you."

Rising to get a beer out of the small refrigerator under the bar, Kerry muttered more to himself than CJ, "You'll wish you'd said yes to the beer in the morning."

"Kerry, you're a man. Tell me. What is a man to do?"

"Oh, no. We're already to Philosophical CJ? That means I missed Fun CJ and Overly Affectionate CJ. He's one of my favorites, by the way. I see it's going to be a long night." Resigned to his fate, Kerry took a seat across the large coffee table and rested his feet on the edge.

CJ ignored his brother's mocking tone. "What did I ever do? To her, I mean."

"I know who you mean. You didn't do anything."

"Exactly!" Now CJ was pointing his index finger, the remaining ones still firmly wrapped around the Glenfiddich bottle.

Kerry rolled his eyes.

"I want to do everything. I want it like I've never wanted anything. And like I've always wanted. Damn it, Kerry. I'm so fucking in love with her, and she won't let me show her."

"Have you tried?"

CJ made to speak, but Kerry cut him off. "Not physically, asshole. Have you tried to get to know her again? Maybe spent some time talking over a nice meal instead of expecting her to fall in line with your teenage plan. She's not the same person who left here those years ago. Have you given her credit for those years?"

"She keeps telling me the same thing. Did she talk to you?" CJ's words were beginning to slur just enough for Kerry to recognize his level of inebriation. He needed to make his point quickly, before the Scotch took CJ under for good.

"Listen to me now, CJ. She doesn't need a grand gesture. She needs you to care about who she is now. Not who you were or what you were then. She's a mom, a teacher, and a widow. You can't erase the last one no matter what you do. She doesn't want to live her life again, to run away with you instead of Jamie. She wants to go forward. You need to help her move forward if you want to be with her when she does. She is, you know, moving forward. She's packing up Jamie's apartment tomorrow, and then she's going to North Carolina."

CJ looked up, sober enough to hear his brother's clear words. "She's leaving? Again?"

"She's not leaving, jackass… She's living. You're the one stuck in the past. Get over yourself, CJ. Quit wallowing. She's not, and she has every reason to wallow. Show her a future, brother." Kerry stood and took the bottle from CJ's hand. He placed it carefully on the bar before returning to help his brother up to a bed – any bed in the family home that didn't currently have a body in it. He had minimal sympathy for the hangover his younger brother would feel in the morning. He'd deny it if asked, but he did acknowledge more sympathy for the heartbreak he knew was at the core.

On reaching the second-floor guest room bed, CJ fell fully clothed onto the soft comforter. "Thanks, Kerry. You're a good brother."

"Oh, no. We've reached Sappy CJ. You stay in this bed. Pass out. Go nowhere." Kerry pointed his index finger at his younger brother.

"Yes, sir. I'm not sure I could if I tried. I love her. And the little one too."

"I know, CJ. Go to sleep."

Kerry slid out of the room and clicked the door shut behind him. "God help us all if she says no."

Chapter 8

Natalie happily joined Sam on the swings at the park around the corner from Molly's apartment. Molly had cheerfully agreed to keep Natalie while Hailey and Amy cleaned up Jamie's old apartment for the afternoon. It was her last task before heading home. Well, not her last, but CJ was going to take more than boxes and a permanent marker to shut down.

She thought she had no choice. It was too hard to look at him and not see the teenager she had been. She had to move on with her life, with Natalie's life. That was what her brain said. Her body betrayed her mind. She felt the slow, sweet ache to be back in his arms, even just to be comforted by those elegant hands moving amiably through her hair. And to feel those lips move against her own…

"Hey, you ready? Where is your head right now?" Amy dropped into the passenger's seat of the borrowed Audi SUV and stared at the smirk on her sister's face.

Amy was wearing a short red and white striped sundress and ballet slipper sandals. She exuded all things fresh and young, two things Hailey knew she herself would not be again.

"I'm here. You look cute. A little too cute for packing and shipping duty today."

"It's about ninety degrees out here. This was the coolest thing I had. Don't blame me if I out-cuted you today. I'm still looking for my Mr. Wonderful."

"And you think I've found mine? Please, Amy."

"I know he's found you. Don't deny it, love. Don't deny yourself. It's okay to feel something for someone other than Natalie."

"You have no idea what you're talking about."

"I know what I saw yesterday. And I know you, big sister. You won't let yourself go there. You should. But you won't."

Hailey knew she'd just been dreaming of going there.

"You and Jamie weren't in the same state, let alone in a good marriage, for the last year. It's time to move on. Past time. Now, let's get this done."

More than a little flustered, Hailey started the car and waved one last time to Natalie before pulling into Chicago traffic. They rolled down the windows and listened to some nineties favorites as they moved slowly through downtown congestion. It was almost like being teenagers again, out in Dad's car on a summer afternoon. They used to go to the beach or one of the museums. Those were good times in a happy childhood. Hailey missed her sister more having had time with her again. She missed this home.

Eventually, she found the building and parked in the underground lot reserved for the apartment residents.

"I brought some boxes and packing tape. They're in the back." Distracted by the details of the day, she and Amy both missed the two men in worn suits leaving the garage stairs just as the women entered.

"Did Jamie buy this place?" They talked as they climbed the two flights of stairs in the late-August heat.

"No, it's part of the job package. It's owned by Wallace Security." Hailey passed a stack of boxes to Amy as she searched her overly large purse for the key.

"You could store a minimart in that thing." Amy shook her head.

"I think I have, especially when Nat was a baby. Jamie used to tease that his entire pack could fit…" She cut off as she pushed the door open to find everything in the apartment upended. Clothes, books, electronics – nothing was where he'd left it.

"Jamie was never neat, but what the hell?" Amy cautiously stepped over the clothes and books on the floor to enter the room, looking around to be sure no one was there.

"Amy, I came here before the funeral to get his things. It was a mess, but not like this. This… is different. Someone was in here. Someone was looking for something."

"Should we call the police?" Amy started to pull her cell phone from her purse.

"I'm not sure I'd know if they found what they came for or if they took anything else. I don't know what was here to start with." Hailey remembered the conversation with Kyle Collinsworth. She'd call him when she got back to the Montgomerys' house.

Amy put away the phone. "Let's close the door and start to get to the bottom of it. Looks like my Mr. Wonderful will have to wait a little longer for our dream date. We could be here a while." As she started to close the door, CJ arrived with two coffee cups in hand. "Oh, wait, here he is now."

"Don't yell, Amy. My brain is screaming already." CJ leaned forward and clung to her before handing over the first cup of coffee.

"You look like you could use it more than me." She giggled loudly, then softer when he shot her a disgusted look.

"I've already had three. That's how I'm standing upright at this moment. Here, Hailey. This one's for you. I came to help, if that's okay."

Hailey took the proffered cup and inhaled the scent. "Mmm, hazelnut. My favorite."

"I know." He said it loud enough that she could hear him, but spoke mostly to himself. "What happened in here? Were you guys looking for something?"

"It wasn't us. And it wasn't this way last week when I came to get Jamie's things. Why do you think someone would be in here?" Hailey carefully stepped over to the bed, pulled the mattress down, and sat on the edge.

"Let's start packing up, and maybe we'll find out." CJ took a large cardboard box and folded it carefully. "What do you want to do with all this stuff?"

Hailey looked around slowly. "Donate it mostly. I'll gather the few things I want to ship home, but most of it was bought here. It's not mine. I'll spare your delicate senses this afternoon and clean out the fridge myself." She smirked, quietly knowing that she was the reason he'd turned to the Scotch last night and felt so wretched today. Well, he deserved a little of it – the miserable, pushy, gorgeous bastard. Sorting through the fridge would give her time to think alone.

By late afternoon, they had dropped off six boxes at the donation center and about fifteen loads to the dumpster. She wasn't even sure what some of the food she'd found in the refrigerator had been originally. Most was now fuzzy, foul-smelling paste. They hadn't found anything of real interest or any answers to who would care about Jamie's things. She packed one box to ship home. *Home*, she reflected. North Carolina was now her home. She worked there, had given birth there. It was the only home Natalie knew. How could it feel so foreign? She'd only left it a little more than two weeks ago. She knew it would always be missing something now.

She hugged Amy before putting her in a cab. She felt sore and sticky. All Hailey wanted now was a cold shower and a crisp glass of wine with her feet up. *No luck there*, she thought as she remembered she had to pick up Nat before driving the SUV back to the Montgomerys' estate. CJ entwined his hand in hers as they walked into the parking garage.

"Did you drive?" She glanced around as if she would know what kind of car he drove. She quickly came to the realization that she knew very little about his life.

"I walked. I don't live far from here. Would you like to come by? I'd like to show you my home. I can offer air conditioning and a cold drink." With a smile, he tugged the keys from her hand and opened the passenger-side door for her.

"Just for a minute. I have to get Natalie."

"Okay."

They drove in silence, both in their own heads. CJ found a spot on the street to park and pulled smoothly to the curb. He took her hand again as they entered the elevator. Her mind shouted, *Danger!* but her heart rose with the short ride. He never took his moss-green eyes off hers as they moved closer to his home. Soft tingles ran down her spine, ended by the ding of the elevator as they reached his floor and finally broke the connection.

His loft was exquisite. She knew it would be. It was elegant, smart, rich, warm – it fit him perfectly.

"I have water or iced tea," CJ said, his head inside the refrigerator.

"Iced tea, unsweet. Thanks."

"I know."

"You say that, and it makes me feel like I'm the most predictable person on the planet." She huffed as she sat on the leather sofa.

CJ handed her the ice-cold glass. "Not predictable. Just comfortable in who you are. No need to change."

"Oh, but I have. In so many ways."

"I want to know about them. I want to share in them. Have dinner with me, Hailey. We'll order in Chinese from Panda House. You always loved them. We'll eat, and we'll get to know each other again." He had the face of an angel, but she knew she might not be able to avoid the devil.

"I have to get Natalie." Hailey pulled out her phone to check for any messages.

"Call Molly. I'm sure she'd keep her or drop her with my mom. She'd love to spend more time with Nat." He stepped in front of her, a little close for her unsteady breathing.

"I've got nothing to change into, and I'm a mess."

CJ shook his head. "What you've got are a bunch of excuses. You know we need to talk. There has to be something in that enormous suitcase you call a purse."

There was. But she didn't have to admit it. "Fine. I'll call Molly. Just dinner." She picked up her phone and wandered into the kitchen space to dial.

∽

CJ disappeared into the bedroom for a quick, and very cold, shower. He returned looking refreshed, calm, and completely in charge. Looks could be deceiving.

Hailey ran a gentle hand over her daughter's crayon drawing attached by a Chicago skyline magnet to CJ's refrigerator, but she dropped her hand and turned as he entered. "It's all set. Nat is going to spend the night at Drew and Jillian's. Apparently, Sam has a bouncy house he's dying to show to Natalie. They're going to have movie night and then camp in the backyard. Jillian said it would be good practice. She's pretty amazing, isn't she? I'm happy for Drew."

CJ loved his sister-in-law now more than ever. "She's the best. If you're staying, why don't you go take a shower? I'll order the food and get it delivered. After what you found in that refrigerator, I'm not cooking. I may not eat, but we'll see." He was forgetting his hangover with each passing minute.

"I can't use your shower." She looked at him in stunned horror.

"Why not?" He threw his hands up in mock surrender. "I'll be good. I have self-control. If you need something to wear, just grab it out of my closet."

CJ watched her war with herself for a moment. Every possible scenario ran across her face. Temptation won out.

"Okay. I won't be long."

"Take your time." He ordered her favorite Chinese, put on the baseball game, and tried his best not to think about what was going on inside his bathroom. He set out informal plates, a glass of crisp white wine for Hailey, and a beer for himself. He started thinking. He'd go easy tonight, not push. Get her talking, find out what she wanted going forward. No pressure. He'd try not to touch her; otherwise, he'd just drive himself crazy.

Then she was there, standing in his living room in a deep-purple tank top and his black boxer briefs. Her fabulous auburn hair hung wild and wet to her shoulders. "I'm sorry. I just couldn't put the sweaty stuff back on. You didn't have a robe. So…" She raised her arms and then put them back down on her thighs.

"No apology necessary. You are every man's fantasy, Hailey." He forgot his own warning. He wanted to touch her then, to run his hands down her slim little body, to carry her to his bed and make love too long in the waiting.

The buzzer interrupted his thoughts and broke the spell. He smiled. "Food's here, and I put out some wine for you."

The meal was delicious, and the beer peeled away another layer of hangover. It felt good to be so casual again – to sit and talk about anything, everything. They watched a little of the baseball game, but their interests lay with each other. They spoke of the past, of Jamie, but mostly of the future. CJ led the conversation in that direction when it was creeping too close to the sad.

"What will you do in North Carolina?"

"Work. I have a classroom of kids waiting for me to get back. I teach technology at a small elementary school there. I'll take care of Natalie, our house. Move on, I guess."

He toyed with a wild curl that he'd wanted to touch all evening. "What if you didn't go? What if you stayed? Built that life here, near your family, near me."

∞

Oh, boy. Here it is. The talk. She'd worked this through in her head. "It's been good to be here with my family and yours. I'll admit that. But my life is there. It has been for thirteen years." She shifted slightly so that they faced each other. He was so casually beautiful – fast-drying curl at the nape of his neck, tanned skin peeking out of a cool white t-shirt. One hand was draped over the back of the sofa, the other playing little circles on her outstretched leg. CJ might have sensed that she wanted to break the connection. He pressed further.

"What if we had a relationship? What if I've fallen in love with you all over again, not for the teenager you were, but for the woman you are? Would that stop you from leaving?" CJ shifted closer, now under her legs so that she was almost in his lap. He leaned forward so that his warm lips could travel slowly upward. First, her fingertips. Next, her hand, finding that sensitive spot in the center of her palm.

"I figured that you might still be mad at me. I haven't thought this through as much as I thought I'd thought this through."

CJ stopped his slow ascension and looked at her. "Do you not want it? Or you don't want me?"

There he was, the embodiment of temptation itself. Hesitantly, she answered with her heart. "I didn't say that."

"Good." It was all he needed. He leaned over her, wrapped his hand into her curls so that she could not turn away, and stared into her eyes. "Hailey, stay with me. Tonight. Don't think too much. I know you're weighing wrong and right at this moment. Don't worry about tomorrow. Tonight." He pressed his lips to hers, never shifting his gaze, his darkening green eyes seeking acceptance without words.

That was the problem, wasn't it? He wanted her now, or to make up for the past. She needed the future. What would happen when she left tomorrow?

She couldn't think. He wouldn't let her. His deft hands were moving up her thighs, sliding toward her hips, sneaking under her shirt. Where were her own hands? God, they were encouraging him.

They were moving across his firm back, her nails digging in at the shoulder before moving into his hair. Her body had betrayed her again. It was falling into rhythm with his without her mind's last word. What would it have been?

Yes.

○○○

Her scent was intoxicating, which, after last night, shouldn't have been so inviting. She smelled like his body wash from the shower, his detergent from his clothes… his. He'd never wanted or needed her more. But not here, like two teenagers on a basement couch pushing the limits before a parent interrupted. He would take her as a woman, would show her he wanted the woman she'd become. He stood, cradling her in his arms, and carried her toward the bedroom.

"You are so beautiful."

She threw her head back with a self-deprecating grunt.

"No, you don't get to do that. Look at me. Look in my eyes. It's the truth. I've seen you with Natalie. You give her so much. Who gives you what you need? I want to. I want to tell you that you're so goddamn gorgeous I can't help but touch you. That you're stronger than any person I know. That you're loved."

He set her on the bed and knelt on the floor between her knees. Eye to eye, he gave her his beating heart. "Will you let me love you?"

She bent forward, resting her forehead against his chest, and sighed. "I don't ever want to break your heart, CJ. I can't live with that."

"Let me worry about my heart." He raised her eyes to his, and a slow tear rolled down her cheek. He swept it away with his hand. "Let me show you."

He took in the sight of her, there in his space as he'd imagined so many times. "Gorgeous." His breath caught in his chest, clogged there with realization that he was finally free. Free to touch, free to love. After years of anticipation, angst, persuading himself that it would never come so that he could move forward. But this – freedom – this was a drug better than any he could prescribe. His touch was reverent but not cautious. He knew what he wanted. He wanted her to feel as cherished as she was.

She lay before him, the epitome of his fantasies, the future of his reality.

∞

The kisses were slow, deliberate, agonizing. Her heart rolled as pain seared down her chest and into her belly. His soft lips caressed her own, teasing her and satisfying those long-held fantasies at the same time. Anxiety shot down to her toes when his touch grazed the soft skin of her abdomen, when his fingers trailed the sides of her body and tugged the shirt over her head.

Fingertips traced over golden skin flushed by her body's tension, soothed by his care. His palm cupped her small breast, his thumb running over the nipple to tease it upward as his tongue gently teased her mouth. His mouth replaced his thumb as he brought her up onto the bed to cover her with his body and his love. He lavished kisses over her slowly, along her neck to that sweet spot where the collar bone meets the chest, over her breasts with tongue and lips and breath, down her center to the fragrant skin of her belly. He slowly removed her boxers – no, his boxers – and God, wasn't that sexy?

This wasn't awkward teenage touching. It was the touch of a man to a woman. She reveled in its ease.

Moving to her knees in the center of the bed, she pulled at his t-shirt, removing the barrier in one quick tug. Chest to chest, soft to firm, skin to heated skin. She reveled in its tenderness.

He unbuttoned his loose jeans and pulled down the waist and his own boxers with one smooth motion. Barriers gone, he lowered her to her back, slid slowly between her thighs, and was home in one long stroke. She reveled in its heat.

He took his time, working them both up to a peak, pulling back at the top and relishing the feeling before taking them home.

Chapter 9

The harsh knock on the front door jarred Hailey out of her daydream.

CJ had gone to work. He had to make rounds with his team and had his regular surgeries to perform. Hailey hadn't realized he had rearranged his schedule to be with her the last few days. He'd put aside work, which was clearly his passion, one he was skilled at. She had witnessed that first hand. He'd put aside family to spend time with her and Natalie. She knew his family was everything to him. She realized she had not given him credit for those things, nor acknowledged to herself that she'd wanted him to do them so desperately – that she'd needed him to do them.

She reread the sweet note he had left on the kitchen counter.

Don't run.
Don't worry.
Don't forget.
Love,
CJ

She smiled and danced a little toward the door, an obvious (albeit appreciative) mess in her tank top, shorts, and crazy sex hair. Peeping through the hole, she glimpsed Kyle Collinsworth dressed in an official-looking suit and holding up his badge, which she couldn't read through the blurry opening. She didn't need to. She had seen her own badge enough times. A crack opened up in her world, a time machine of memories locked away.

"Hailey? It's Kyle Collinsworth. We need to talk."

Her spirits fell. She released the chain and opened the door slowly. "I was going to call you."

"I'm sorry to catch you at a bad time." He looked her over from tank top to boxers, careful not to linger too long in any one area before awkwardly stepping into the loft. "I waited until Dr. Montgomery was well on his way."

"Can I ask how you knew I was here?" Her face flushed now as she guided him to the large sofa in the living area and signaled him to sit.

"FBI, Hailey. You would know." He appeared frustrated already.

"Right, yes. So, you know about my past, my job before I had Natalie… of my clearance? You've seen my file?" Hailey sat heavily on the sofa near him.

"Yes. Why didn't you share it when I came to see you in the hospital?"

"It's classified. I would expect you know that. I wasn't a field agent either. I worked a listening post and hacked an occasional computer no one knew existed. I don't run around telling everyone I meet for the first time. I closed that box a long time ago. I'm moving on." She looked down at her attire before adding, "Obviously."

"Well, I'm gonna need you to open the box back up. If we're going to sort out what really happened to Jamie."

"How do you know something did happen? What have you got to go on? Wait, no. Don't tell me. If you tell me, then I'm back in. I'm not going to be back in. I have a daughter, a job, a life."

"Here's the thing…"

"No, no, there's no thing!" She waved her index finger at him while swigging a sip of now-cold coffee from the end table.

"The thing is… I think Jamie knew you would be here. I think he knew he could trust you, maybe only you, if something happened."

She got up to pace. And to think. "But why? We'd been apart for so long."

"Yes, that's true. But you'd been together longer. You knew him like no one else – since childhood. And you're smart. Jamie spoke of you often when we would meet."

"I can't believe I'm considering this. Am I considering this?" She tapped her hands over her belly, a gut check of sorts.

"I hope so. I've put my butt on the line and pulled some strings. Please say you are considering this." Now Kyle took a swig of the cold coffee.

"I swore I would never go back to that life. Alone for so many years. My family didn't even know what I did. I have Natalie to think of now. And CJ? I need a minute here."

Kyle peered down at his linked fingers. "Yeah, about CJ... You can't tell him about any of this. What I've got so far is confidential, especially when it comes to Dr. Montgomery. I understand that you have a connection to him... to his past."

Slowly, with the help of this virtual stranger in front of her, she realized the truth. "I don't just have a connection to his past. I have a connection to his future."

"Well, he may be involved in this in a roundabout way, and we need to make sure he won't go to his father with this information."

"His father? JP Montgomery? How is he involved in anything?" She slowly sat back down next to Kyle.

"He may or may not be involved. We can work through all of it if you've decided to join me."

"I don't see that I have any other choice at this point. You are a very talented man, Kyle Collinsworth."

"Thank you, Hailey."

Hailey looked into his kind grey eyes. "Who did this to Jamie?"

"I'm not sure yet. Jamie gave us some information that someone inside Wallace Security is helping to move contraband into the city. Maybe even running the operation. It's not clear yet. We didn't move on anyone at Jamie's request. He was gathering information to bring down the whole ring. All I can figure is that Jamie must have figured out who was involved but he never got the chance to tell me before he died. I think whoever it is pushed Jamie off that building at the port."

"Okay, now you're scaring me. Not sure I want to be in on this. Oh, I found something at his apartment." She got up to find her purse. "It's a flash drive that was inside a jewelry box for Natalie. I haven't seen what's on it. I don't have a computer." She was frustrated at first that she couldn't find the drive amongst gummy bear wrappers and half-used lipstick containers. Then she remembered. "I left it at the Montgomerys."

"What? Are you kidding me? That could be evidence."

"Well, I didn't know that. I'll get it later today. No one knows it's there or suspects anything other than an accident. I'll get it."

A solid knock had Hailey jumping in her seat. "Shit. That's Amy."

Kyle put his hand on her knee to steady her. "I'll go."

He peered through the small hole in the center but pulled back quickly. "Wow." Rubbing his hands together, he gripped the knob and opened the large loft door.

"Who are you?" Amy pushed into the room. Hailey watched as Kyle simply stared back at her as if distracted by something unseen. "You speak English, buddy? Habla inglés?"

Snapped back to reality, he answered carefully, "Hablo inglés y español. And Mandarin, Portuguese, and Arabic."

"Well… thank you for your resume. Is my sister here?" Amy cocked her head to the side.

"Your sister? Yes. You're Amy Wilks?"

"Who's asking? And how do you know my name?"

"Kyle Collinsworth, ma'am." He held out a hand to shake hers and then pulled back in mock surrender after receiving her glare. "I come in peace."

"Ma'am?" Amy gave an involuntary hiss.

"What is it with you two? It's a term of respect. At least, it's meant to be."

"It makes me feel like an old maid."

Kyle shook his head slowly. "You are anything but that."

She smiled. "I'm going to take that as a compliment, as I'm sure it was intended, and find my sister, sir." She rolled her eyes and turned toward the room.

Kyle quietly closed the door. Hailey chuckled as Amy moved closer.

"Hailey, are you okay? Where's CJ? And who is this guy?" Amy turned back toward the door where Kyle remained, fixed and apparently fascinated.

"I see you met Kyle, with the eyes."

"Yeah. The same grey eyes as the police officer who just stopped me for speeding my way to you. That hundred is going to hurt my budget for awhile. If he hadn't been so damned good looking, I'd have unleashed my wrath at his ill timing, like with this poor schmuck." Amy cocked her thumb in the general direction of Kyle. "Instead, I went for the shy, helpless female bit. Not that it has ever been effective. I am rightly removing it from my female toolbox." She shook her head. "Never again."

"Well, this set of grey eyes seems to be aroused by the wrath." Hailey pointed quickly toward Kyle who hadn't taken his eyes off Amy since she had arrived.

"Hailey, what is going on here? This better not be… I know I'm not here for a set-up."

"No, although it's now a thought. Kyle was in Jamie's platoon. He's a good guy. And he was just leaving."

Kyle took the cue given to him. "Right. Hailey, I'll be in touch. You have my cell if anything comes up." Kyle nodded toward the two women. "Ma'am." He was smiling as he left. Amy groaned loudly from inside the loft.

"I think he likes you." Hailey giggled as she headed into the bedroom.

"Yeah, great. Am I taking you to the airport later?"

"Uh… No. Change of plans. Did you bring me the clothes I asked for? I'm not taking the walk of shame I might have in high school."

"Yeah, I brought you a sundress."

"I'll try to fit into your size. I think you have lost weight in school. I'm worried about you."

"Well, I've been busy. No worries. Are you okay?"

Hailey flashed a smile as she took the clothes from Amy. "I need to go run some errands and pick up Natalie. I think I'll stay a bit longer."

"Does this have anything to do with the boxer shorts you're wearing?"

Hailey answered, "Partially. Don't ask yet, Amy. I'm not sure what is happening. All I know today is that I need to buy a laptop."

❦

Lilac-scented breeze moved over her shoulders, summer sun baked the toenail polish peeking out of her sandals, and memories flooded back. She sat on the small deck just off her bedroom at the Montgomery Estate. By Natalie's report, the sleepover had been the ultimate – movie, popcorn, bounce house, and sleeping in a tent outside. Hailey reflected on her own sleepover – baseball, Chinese food, sex, and sleeping in a world of questions. Both now feeling the effects of their respective evenings, Natalie was napping on the bed inside while Hailey was inserting the flash drive she'd found at Jamie's apartment into her new computer. Memories of late-night college studying, coding exams, and hacking parties raced through her brain. She'd been recruited to the FBI in her last semester of college. Husband abroad, she'd swooned over the flattery and the opportunity to help, if only in a small way and from afar.

She opened the drive to find one scanned file. It was titled "Shipments" and contained a list of six dates, written in Jamie's chicken-scratch handwriting. There were both past and future dates, with an upcoming September 6th of this year highlighted. *What was Jamie keeping this for? What was he trying to figure out? What would happen on that day? What would make this worth a life?*

Natalie opened the sliding door and sleepily pulled herself into Hailey's lap. "Snuggles, Mama."

"Of course, baby." Hailey closed the laptop and pushed it onto the small table in front of them. "Ready for some dinner?"

"Yep. Are we going home?"

Hailey shuddered out a breath. Her insightful daughter always seemed to know what was on her own mind. "I'm not sure when, baby. Do you miss home?"

Natalie nodded. "But I like it here."

Hailey added, "Me too. Now, let's get some food. I bet Ms. Anna has something yummy in the fridge."

※

CJ's return to work had been just what he'd needed. He'd missed the routine of it, the grounded nature of the job, and the high of a save. He had done two scheduled surgeries and helped with a trauma call down where he'd saved a little girl from losing her spleen after a car accident. She wasn't much bigger than Natalie and with just as much spunk. He had walked home on a high. While initially disappointed to find his apartment empty, he was reassured to find the note from Hailey that she would be at his parents' home. It soothed his nerves somewhat, but not the itch to see her.

After a shower and a shave, CJ opened the front door of the Montgomery house and snuck inside. Why did he feel like a teenager? He was an adult, a surgeon, and he'd done nothing wrong. He had snuck in so many times in high school that the time of night and the nature of his visit had him reminiscing – until he felt the eyes upon him.

His mom sat in the quiet study off the entry, under the light of a small floor lamp, reading a book. Or she had been before he'd crept in the front door.

Andrea slowly returned her attention to her lap as if she hadn't seen him and cleared her throat. "She's gone to bed already. Both of them have." Andrea put her reading glasses back on and pretended she was interested in the book.

"Hi, Mom. How do you know I haven't come to see you?" CJ walked quietly toward her and leaned down for a hug.

"Because you never come to see me and I've spotted you sneaking in that front door more times than I can count. Granted, it was usually after some illicit escapade rather than toward one, but the look is pretty much the same." She gave him a wry smile.

"Illicit? Only that one time." He laughed quietly; the peace of the house seemed to expect it.

"How are you? How was work?" Andrea gently patted the ottoman in front of her, inviting him to sit.

"It's all good, Mom. Listen, I know the subtext here. You don't need to check on me... or us."

"Is there an us now? Last I saw you, Hailey was crying, and you were partaking of too much of Dad's Glenfiddich."

Nausea returned. "Don't remind me. We haven't sorted 'us' out yet. I'm just trying hard to be here for her, to be what she needs."

"Are you now? And what is that? Tell me. What does she need?"

"A friend."

"And?" Andrea raised her eyebrows imperceptibly.

"Mom. I'm not having this conversation with you."

"I know you've spent a long time thinking about her, about a relationship with her. What does she want? Have you asked?" Andrea crossed her legs on the ottoman next to CJ, as if she had these kind of conversations every day. CJ shifted slightly.

"We're working it out. I don't think she knows exactly what she wants yet."

"But you know what you want?"

"Absolutely. Her. I've always wanted her. I'm willing to wait for her to see that, to see me."

"And if she doesn't see it? If she doesn't love you? What will you do?"

"Aren't you the one who told me that love finds a way? We'll find a way." He kissed her forehead as he stood up. "I'll just pop up and say goodnight, then."

"Uh huh." She returned to her book.

"I love you, Mom."

"Uh huh."

CJ backed out of the room and took the stairs two at a time, but he didn't get away fast enough to miss his mom's final thoughts.

"Be careful, son."

Shadows filled the hallway as light from Natalie's nightlight spilled out of her room. He thought to tiptoe by but heard a faint whisper of his name from inside.

"CJ? CJ? Come in my room!"

He pushed the door open and snuck into the space. "Why are you up? You should be sleeping."

'Shhh! Don't talk too loud. Mama will hear us. I wanted to see you. Will you read me a story?"

"Just a quick one." He turned on the bedside light. "Scoot over, kiddo. How about this one?" He sat by the edge of the big queen-sized bed, leaned against the headboard, and melted as Natalie snuggled in next to him to listen.

"Mama read this one tonight. I know all the pictures."

"What's it about?"

"Mary and her sheep. One gets lost. See, it's soft here." She raised her hand to the book and rubbed two small fingers over the cotton puff standing up above the pages.

"I like this kind of book." He slowly read each page of the board book, stopping to pet the sheep or feel the ticklish grass. He rested his hand on Natalie's soft hair, so similar to Hailey's. What a miracle she was, so smart and kind. He marveled at her fortitude, having lost her dad such a short time before. After several minutes without hearing her add in her own take on the pages of the book, CJ peeked over her drooping head to find she was asleep.

Careful not to disturb what must have been dreams of diamond tiaras and fountains full of glitter, he shifted off the bed and turned off the light. Shadows fell across her face, peaceful and quiet.

One room over, Hailey's door lay cracked open. He closed it behind him as he entered, moving toward the open French doors and billowing curtains. Hailey leaned against the railing of the deck, her nightgown flowing in the gentle breeze, the outline of her body beneath shadowed from the moonlight above. This was what he wanted: to come home to this, to be needed here and to need in return. Hailey turned her head with a sleepy smile as he reached the doorway.

"Hi. Didn't expect you tonight. I thought you were working."

He stopped behind her, slid his arms around her waist, and began kissing her neck, feeling desire rise within him. "I did. I'm done. I wanted you." Each word was followed by a gentle kiss as he traveled a lazy path from neck to shoulder and then slowly back.

"CJ, I… want you too. But Natalie… she's next door. I'm not sure…"

"Asleep. I just read her a book and tucked her back in. She's out." CJ watched a kind of peace fall over Hailey at the thought of her daughter safe and thriving. She turned into his embrace. He stopped only long enough to find her lips and tug her into the room.

This Hailey was gentle, somehow freer than she could be in day-to-day life. She gave, and he took.

His pulse was slow. This rhythm was easy. This was right. He untied the string between her shoulders, and the straps slipped down. One last tug, and the gown fell softly to the floor. Moonlight and the smell of lilacs captured the room.

"I want you to know how beautiful you are. I should have told you every day. I regret so much. Mostly that you would ever think I didn't need you or want you like this."

"We were teenagers, CJ."

"And now here we are. I don't want to regret anything about this time. I want to be honest with you. To tell you I need you. I don't want you to go." He caressed her shoulders and then ran his hands through her hair as he talked.

"No regrets."

"No regrets." He coaxed her forward as he removed his clothes and pulled the covers aside. Sitting, bared in chest and soul, he leaned forward and kissed the soft area between her breasts. She let her head fall back as he moved to her breast, weighing each in his firm hands, rounding down to her hips before pulling her onto his lap. They matched, chest to chest, heartbeat to heartbeat. No, he would not let her go without a fight this time. He wanted her to really see him, perhaps for the first time.

"Open your eyes, Hailey. Show me." Spurred on by his words, she raised her hips up and slid down, meeting his gaze directly. She moved, and he matched, power to power, until they both had no regrets.

Chapter 10

Tiptoeing into the office space, Hailey felt out of place, out of her depth, and, in all probability, out of her mind. *Oh God, what have I agreed to?*

She had convinced herself in the wee hours of the night that she could do anything, pumped herself up like an Olympic swimmer about to dive into clear water. Now she was sure she was drowning.

The appointment had been easy enough to obtain. *Check.* No one suspected her true motives. *Check.* She had thrown up in the bathroom before breaking out in hives from head to toe. *Check and Check.*

She'd told herself this wouldn't take more than a few days to clear up, not more than a few hours on her new shiny computer to hack, not more than a week to right this ship that had become her life. *God, I hope it's not the Titanic.*

The investigation had to start somewhere – Wallace Security's home offices and the president himself was as good a place as any.

Knocking on his open door, she said, "Hello… Mr. Wallace? It's Hailey Powers, sir."

The old man popped up from behind a pile of papers, reminding Hailey of Nat's jack-in-the-box toy she'd tripped over more times than she could count. "Oh, Miss. Of course, of course. Please come in and sit with me. I'll move some paperwork around. Please, sit here."

Mr. Wallace pointed toward a small armchair directly across from his desk. At least, she assumed a desk lay under the piles of papers, folders, and boxes in front of him. Sheldon Wallace stood to shake her hand and guide her through the space. He wore a tweed jacket with felt elbow patches, no tie, and penny loafers, while his white hair stood on end as if a Chicago wind had just blown through that instant. Perhaps that would explain the chaos. His handshake was firm, weathered like his skin, and he smelled of cigars and peppermint.

"Thank you. The flowers you sent for my husband's funeral were just lovely."

"Flowers? Hold on." He pushed the plastic intercom on his desk. "Melanie, did we send flowers for the Powers funeral?"

The intercom hissed. "Of course, sir. Do you need coffee, sir?"

"Yes, that would be nice." He put his hand over the speaker and leaned toward Hailey. "You drink coffee, dear? Or tea? We have tea."

"Coffee would be lovely. Thank you."

He yelled back to the competent Melanie, who probably didn't need the intercom to hear his requests, as her desk was situated just outside. Hailey had noted her immaculate desk as she'd entered, making the disarray inside all the more jarring.

"I'll be in with coffee, sir."

"Yes, well, now that the formalities are taken care of, I want to say how sorry we are about your husband's fall. I just can't see how it might have happened. No, I just can't see. We pride ourselves on training our employees well. Terrible accident. Yes, terrible."

He appeared to be muttering more to himself than Hailey as Melanie entered with the coffee. *How does this man run a multimillion dollar company? With pen and paper, apparently. And Melanie probably runs the place. The problem? First rule of hacking: you need a computer to hack. Not one in sight.*

This was going to be more challenging than she'd anticipated. Hailey smiled as Melanie winked at her and served Mr. Wallace a cup of coffee.

"Sir, did you ever meet my husband?"

"Yes, yes, I did. He came through here regularly. Strapping young man, but you already know that. I try to keep my finger on the pulse of my own company. I know they mock me for my system in here, but it works for me. Put my kids through college and bought my wife a nice new Cadillac last year. Yes, I keep up with my employees. Your husband did his job well, and I can appreciate that. Now, we need to talk about the insurance. Yes, you must be taken care of."

"Mr. Wallace. There's no need…"

"Yes, yes, there is. He did good work. Do you have children?"

Hailey sighed but raised a weak smile. "We have a daughter, Natalie. She's almost five."

"Well, there you go. Natalie will need to be taken care of. Let me just find the paperwork. Melanie! Where is the damn insurance paperwork for the Powers family?"

"Sir, really, we don't need…" Hailey felt her hives returning.

"Ah, here it is! The policy pays out a million dollars."

"Excuse me, sir?" Hailey almost spit out her coffee. Her eyes darted around the room to find help or hidden cameras.

"I said it pays a million dollars. I just need to find a pen." He patted his shirt pocket and then down to his pants. "Melanie! I need a pen!"

"Sir, I can't take your money. You didn't cause this. I didn't come here expecting this…" Hailey set down her coffee with a shaking hand, making the china cup skitter on the plate.

"That's why we have insurance! I pay them enough. 'Bout time they came through. We'll take care of it, dear. I promise."

Melanie entered, trying to contain a laugh, with Scott close behind. "Sir, Mr. Cannon is here to meet with you. I'll escort Mrs. Powers out."

"Yes, yes. We'll take care of it. You go be with your sweet Natalie. Melanie will take care of you. So sorry, dear. And hello, Scott. We have much to discuss."

Scott appeared to be surprised at Hailey's presence. "Hailey, nice to see you. What are you doing here?"

"I met with Mr. Wallace… briefly. He has been so kind."

"He is that." Lowering his voice so that only she could hear, he continued. "And quirky, and hectic, and occasionally over-caffeinated.

Do you need something? I know it can be difficult to hold a directed conversation with the man."

The pressure building in her chest had her stumbling for an explanation. "I just wanted to meet him and thank him for the flowers."

"Did he know that he had sent them?" Scott sent a knowing smile down at her.

The pressure valve released a little with the joke. "Melanie was very helpful."

"She is that. She is his granddaughter. Did you know that? She has an MBA, and I'm pretty sure she runs this place most days."

"Ah, that makes more sense. Would she be my contact from human resources, then? I need to find out which bank Jamie had been using for his paycheck. Anyway, so sorry to slow you down. Thanks for the information. I'll let you two meet." Hailey turned to say goodbye, but Mr. Wallace was back behind his wall of papers and appeared to be in deep concentration over a handwritten spreadsheet.

"Hailey?"

She turned back toward Scott, who was standing just an inch closer than she expected. Looking up into his light eyes, she answered. "Yes."

"If you need anything else, just call. Okay?"

She couldn't help herself. "Actually… no, never mind."

"What is it, Hailey?"

"Would you have any interest in… a date?" She raised her eyebrows, enjoying the craft of matchmaking.

"But I thought… you and CJ…"

"Oh! No, not me. Sorry. With my sister, Amy. She's single, and you're single, and I just thought, maybe…"

"That would be great. Sure. Just call my secretary to set it up."

"Call your secretary? Alrighty, then." Before she had a chance to clarify further, Mr. Wallace waved Scott over for their meeting, and Melanie escorted her toward the door.

"Melanie, right? Thank you for your help today. I just need to find Jamie's last paystub. His apartment is a bit… disorganized, as you might understand." Hailey shrugged and laughed. Melanie rolled her eyes in agreement, as this was her daily life.

"Sure. Of course. I have a file here. I'll make you a copy." Melanie moved toward a set of sleek, low filing cabinets behind her desk. Reaching for the first set, she immediately located the document and laid it quietly on the copy machine. "Will you be staying in Chicago long? Or are you headed home soon?"

Hailey lingered on the word home. Chicago had been home for so many years, and then North Carolina. *Now what? Was Carolina home anymore? Was anywhere?*

She came back to reality as Melanie swore at the copy machine and gave it a smack. "Blasted thing! Always pulls the paper in at a weird angle. I think it still has all the information you need, just looks a little wonky. The corner is folded, but it looks like Chicago National is your bank. Maybe your next stop?" Melanie sat gracefully as she handed over the document.

"Yes, thank you. I appreciate your help." She scurried out before her hives returned. Deep breaths. Her first foray as investigator had led her to nothing of note. Well, except more questions… and a million dollars.

Ironically, Adele's theme song from *Skyfall* played through the speakers as Hailey waited for the Chicago National Bank representative to assist her. She'd found the bank just down the street from Jamie's apartment and figured the key attached to the flash drive must have been for a safety deposit box in the same location. She'd even surprised herself when she'd walked up to the teller and requested admission to the vault and the box. Now she waited, with Natalie at her side, anticipating a rejection. Natalie placed her hand on Hailey's knee to stop it from bouncing, as Hailey had done so many times to her before.

"Here she comes, Mommy. She's pretty."

"Yes, she is."

The bank attendant approached and handed Hailey back her identification along with Jamie's death certificate. "Everything is in order. Do you have your key?"

"Yes, thank you."

"Then follow me."

They walked down a quiet hallway to the room of boxes, with a high table centered amongst them. Hailey thought it all felt very

James Bond-ish, but the attendant appeared bored. Just another day in the bank. Hailey couldn't help but surmise what would be in the box. Paperwork? Jewelry? Flash drive number one?

The attendant left them alone in the room after removing box number 617 and placing it on the table. Hailey dug through her purse to find the flash drive attached to the key. She was going to solve mysteries today. At least, that is what she told herself. Pressing the key into the lock, she turned and lifted the lid slowly.

Really? One piece of paper? It was some kind of ledger. The one-page document was an invoice from Montgomery Shipping tallying the cargo weight on a freighter that entered the Port of Chicago on May 18th of this year. Nothing else. Nothing on the back side, no code, no handwriting. No flash drive labeled number one either. No other paperwork. What was so special about this piece of paper that Jamie had kept it so particularly secure?

Nat interrupted her thoughts. "Mama, I have to go to the bathroom." She did a little dance in her Mary Jane's.

"Right. Okay. Let's go." Hailey put the paper in her purse and closed the box. If she was James Bond – and at this point, she sure didn't feel much like him – then she had the cutest Bond girl ever by her side. "Bathroom, then dinner."

"Can it be ice cream?" Natalie smiled brightly – the Mind Bender this time. It was no use fighting it.

"Roger that."

Chapter 11

"Bowling? Really? I can't picture your dad bowling." Hailey chuckled at the thought of the upstanding, proper millionaire that was JP Montgomery pulling on rented shoes and throwing a bowling ball down the lane.

"He loves it, actually. He was the one who had the matching shirts made." CJ laughed out loud with Hailey. "I checked with Ms. Anna. She would be happy to babysit Natalie. I'm officially inviting you to Montgomery Men's Night as my guest."

"But it's Men's Night." Hailey added extra reverence for effect.

"So. Jillian played poker with us. Mom has gone out on the boat with us. It's not totally unprecedented. Although it does solidify your special place in this family." CJ smiled and put his arm around Hailey's shoulders. "I believe you even came to one back in high school."

"I remember. Probably better than you." She laced her fingers with his. "You held my hand."

"I remember just fine. You were so pretty that night. The light-blue shirt you wore turned your eyes the bluest I'd ever seen them. I wanted to steal you away. Just like I do now." Turning her into his arms, he lifted her chin, and her eyes met his. The kiss was quiet and coaxing. His hands moved slowly to the back of her neck so the soft hair there fell over them. She opened for him. Her tongue tasted of tea and honey. This was what he had wanted then. This was what he wanted now.

"Fine. You've seduced me. I'll bowl."

After settling Natalie in with Ms. Anna for some baking fun, they were the last to arrive at the lanes. Kerry and Drew laughed over open beers while wearing matching green bowling shirts with bright white trim, nicknames sprawled across the right chest on each.

JP shook CJ's hand. "Where is your shirt, Middle Man?"

Hailey looked up at CJ and smiled. "Middle Man?"

"It says Dr. Middle Man actually. You know, middle child and all. I left it at the loft, Dad. I… didn't want Hailey to feel left out." His brothers laughed.

"I could have gotten one for you, Hailey, had my son told me you were coming." CJ brushed off the usual fatherly disdain from JP. "Would have put Little Mama on the pocket." JP smiled and rested his hand on her shoulder.

Kerry chimed in, "If we're done talking fashion, ladies, can we bowl now? Losers buy the next round." Hailey noted his shirt said "Kerry On."

She nodded. "High-stakes bowling. Got it. I'm going for rented shoes and a stiff drink. Can I bring you back anything, Dr. Middle Man?" Hailey giggled as Kerry rolled his impatient eyes.

"Sure. I'll take a beer. Got my own shoes." He winked as she moved away toward concessions.

Drew spoke up. "So… invitation to Men's Night is usually reserved for a sparse few. Does this mean she's staying? Did someone get lucky?"

"Shut up, Baby Drew. You'll be lucky if I don't kick your ass."

Drew laughed at him. "You doth protest too much, brother."

Kerry stepped between the two. "And if you ladies are done with the psychoanalysis, can we please bowl?"

"Yes. Baby Drew and Kerry On against Hailey and me. I'll even throw in Dad on your side."

"That's because he doesn't contribute anything, unless we put the blow-up gutter guards in again." All three brothers laughed.

JP stood up and snatched a ball from the return. "I've contributed plenty to you boys. I don't need your pity." The bang of the ball landing on the wooden lane stifled their laughter, which resumed when only a single pin fell at the end.

"Shush."

◠◡◠

Hailey sat to put on the worn tan and teal rented shoes. She watched as JP's second ball ended up in the gutter. He fell into the plastic chair next to her with a huff.

She glanced up and felt a small pang of pity. "It just takes practice and patience. I'm sure you'll be throwing strikes by the end of the night."

He whispered back, "I'll let you in on my secret. Don't tell CJ."

Hailey sighed and thought there was a lot of that going on in her life.

"I only let them think I'm bad at it. I can bowl. I just like to have them all together. I enjoy watching them bond over it."

"What? You're faking it? What else are you hiding, Mr. Montgomery?" Hailey stopped tying her shoes and peered up at his tall frame.

"So many things…" With that, he walked over to pick up his beer and keep score.

Hailey remembered back to her childhood. The matchmaker in her had tried to discuss the Montgomery parents many times with the boys. How had they met? Andrea had always been so loving, so giving. JP was tough on them, not unfair, but not friendly either. Was it really opposites attract? Or were they more alike than the kids knew? Hailey was starting to think it was the latter. Then she thought of Kyle's investigation, about his feeling that the person responsible could be close. Could JP Montgomery be the inside man? Could he have pushed Jamie that night or authorized such a thing?

"Hailey!" CJ was yelling her name, bringing her back. "It's your turn. You alright? You're white as a ghost."

"I'm fine." Her eyes locked on CJ's. "Really. It's time to take these clowns down. Hold my beer."

CJ just smiled. In the end, it came down to the last frames for each team. Kerry hit nine pins on his first throw and then picked up the spare. It was up to her. She turned to watch Kerry high five his dad. She saw a genuine smile from JP crinkling his gentle eyes. This man could not be the one who had torn apart her world. Could he? She put her foot up on the bench to tie her shoelace and to get a pep talk from CJ. "Don't remember those two being so close."

"My dad and Kerry? Well, they work together all day. Their personalities are different, but Kerry is his number two. Now, get in the zone, girl. Let's finish them off."

"Number two?" She stared straight ahead, no longer talking to CJ. "That's it! Number two! I've got to go! I'll catch a cab. See you in the morning."

"What? But we're about to win. Where are you going?" CJ took the beer she handed him as she grabbed her purse and speed-walked out the front door, bowling shoes and all.

"Taxi!" A white and red cab stopped at the curb as she dug through her huge bag to find her cell phone and Kyle's business card. "Buzz On In on State Street, please."

The cab pulled away as she dialed the number. "Kyle? Kyle, it's Hailey. I know who it is. Number two! It's not a number. It's a person!"

Chapter 12

"Meet me at Buzz On In on State Street… Yes, now!" Hailey ended the call and shoved the phone back in her purse, patting it nervously throughout the short trip. Jamie had left her a clue. She just needed to think through all the moving parts. It was simple. Number two.

She paid the cab driver and pushed into the coffee shop. As she looked around, there was no sign of Kyle yet, but she did spy Jillian behind the counter. "Hey, Jillian. How are you?"

"Hi, Hailey. Didn't expect you in here tonight! Mostly college kids and late-night munchies going on in here tonight. What can I get you?"

"I'll take a decaf coffee. I just left Drew at the bowling alley."

Jillian nodded. "Montgomery Men's Night invitation, huh? Why aren't you still there? Did they scare you away?"

"No, I'm meeting someone. I was tired of kicking their butts. They are not good bowlers!"

"So I've heard. But they are pretty cute in their green shirts." Jillian laughed out loud while she prepared Hailey's decaf. "Here you go. On the house."

"Thanks, Jillian." Hailey turned toward the entrance and caught a glimpse of Kyle. He was standing in front of a cab, kissing a woman. Wait, that wasn't 'a woman.' It was Amy! Hailey slid to the side of the window to watch. They had a small conversation and then kissed one more time before Amy got back into the cab.

Kyle went directly to Hailey's table as he entered. "Hailey, what's going on? It sounded urgent on the phone."

"Well, I didn't know you were hot and heavy with my sister at the time. I guess I should have waited until the morning."

"Uh…"

"Wow. Kyle, how did that happen? Last I checked, you two were mocking each other, and she was shooting death rays at you from her eyes."

"Well… I called her. She didn't say no. We went out. I don't need to defend myself here, Hailey."

"No, not from me. Her maybe…"

"I'm a big boy. I can handle myself. But if she asks, I got her number from you, not the FBI database. Now, what is this number two business that I broke my date early to hear?"

"I think the number two written on the flash drive was a clue. I haven't been able to find number one. I thought I must have missed it when I cleaned out Jamie's apartment. But I didn't think hard enough about why it was written in roman numerals. It was a clue. CJ said something tonight about his dad…"

Kyle shifted in his seat. "Wait, I thought we had a deal. What does CJ know?"

"Nothing. I haven't told him anything. But when we were bowling with his dad, he said something…"

"Excuse me? Wait one minute. You were bowling with JP Montgomery? I'd pay money to see that."

"Yeah, I know. Anyway, CJ said his brother Kerry was JP's number two. It sparked this idea. Maybe number two is not a number, but a person. When I had dinner with the family last week, I met another one of JP's business partners. His name is Scott Cannon."

"Yes, high up in Montgomery Shipping. He checked out on my initial searches."

"Yeah, well, did you know he came from a rough part of Chicago and has the roman numeral two tattooed on his hand."

"No, but… that's it? That's what you've got. I go on one date a year, Hailey. One. Tonight, I could be out with your sister, and you had me come here for that. That's not evidence, Hailey. That's coincidence."

"It's a gut feeling. I know he is involved."

"Well, I can't go to a judge for a warrant with a gut feeling. I'm gonna need more actual evidence, Hailey."

"You're the one who said this wasn't an accident. That your gut told you otherwise. This whole thing is based on instinct! There's something else. After the scene outside, I think it may be…"

"What?" Kyle's frustration mounted.

"I kind of set Amy up on a date with him… tomorrow night." Hailey cringed. "It was before all of this or… that." She waved toward the door where she'd witnessed the love scene now burned into her eyes.

"Well, that's not going to happen! Seriously, Hailey. Maybe I shouldn't have pulled you into this. Let me work on things from within the system. Don't do anything stupid, Hailey."

"I could say the same to you, Kyle. My sister will hunt you down and eat you alive."

"Of that, I have no doubt. Now I remember why I don't date anyone. She can't be involved in this."

CJ pulled open the door to Buzz On In.

Hailey's gut dropped. "Shit! This is not happening."

CJ moved straight toward them, his eyes focused on her. "What's not happening? Hailey, what the hell is going on? Who is this guy?"

Hailey took a sip of her coffee and then set it down very slowly. "Did you follow me?"

"Yes. Did you think I wouldn't after you ran out without any explanation?"

Hailey threw her hands in the air as a sign of surrender. "Fine. CJ, meet Kyle. Kyle, meet CJ. Kyle is with the Federal Bureau of Investigation."

"Hailey!" Both men exclaimed in unison.

"Excuse me? FBI? Why?"

"I ask myself that question every day." Kyle walked in a slow circle, as if stalking the situation, deciding how to proceed.

"Hailey, what exactly is going on here?" CJ pulled her elbow to turn her toward him.

"I'm helping Kyle figure out what exactly happened to Jamie. We need to talk. Not here though. I'll meet you at the house."

"I'll wait and take you back myself."

Deep breath. "Fine. Kyle, I'll call you in the morning. Think through what I told you."

∞

CJ refrained from the barrage of questions he had running through his head until they arrived back at the Montgomery House. He'd give Hailey a chance to gather her thoughts and tell him the truth. Then he was going to tell her how things were going to go. She was going to drop any foolish idea of helping the FBI, for God's sake. What was she thinking?

Hailey jumped out of the SUV as he pulled up to the front door. She held up her hand as he got out and started to speak. "Not yet. Not yet. We'll talk, but I'm going to check on Natalie first. I'll meet you in the game room when I'm done." She turned and walked inside without looking back or waiting for his response.

CJ pulled the Scotch off the shelf behind the bar and poured more than he should have into a glass. *FBI? How did she get into this? Sweet Hailey. Why is everything so damn hard when it comes to her?*

She walked in while his back was turned to the door. "Ahem… If I'm going to do this, I'm gonna need one of those drinks first."

CJ poured from the bottle and pushed the glass toward her. "Oh, you're going to do this, alright. Go."

"Where to start? I told you about the baby we lost, about my time in North Carolina."

"Yes. You finished school and started teaching while Jamie was abroad."

She pulled out a bar stool and toed up to sit on it. "This is going to be easier if you just listen. I'll answer your questions, if you have some, after I get it all out."

"Fine. And expect questions."

"Right, yes." She stared down into her glass of Scotch. "During my senior year of college… I was recruited."

"Military recruited?"

"CJ! Let me tell you what I need to tell you." She stood up to pace as she talked.

CJ took his glass and sat heavily on the leather couch. "Sorry. You were recruited…"

"I've told you that I've changed. I'm not the girl who left here those years ago. This is what I became. I was recruited through college and worked for the agency, CJ. I did high-level intelligence monitoring via audio and computer surveillance for six years. I've participated in more shit than you can imagine, here and abroad. I've tried to tell you. I'm not who or what you think I am." She slowly sat down next to him on the couch. "But I walked away. When I got pregnant with Nat, I changed my life. I focused on her alone and waited for Jamie to come home."

"Did Jamie know? He allowed you to do this?"

"Umm… okay, couple things. One, he didn't know because my work was classified, and two, it wasn't 1952. I didn't need his permission to do a job. One I was good at, by the way." Hailey rolled her eyes and then returned her focus to CJ.

"I'm hoping that this is the 'get it all out' part. That you're not about to tell me that you're getting back in."

"I never saw any of this coming. I swore I would never go back. Too much risk but… what I see now…" She pushed to stand again to relieve some of the pressure building in her chest. "Kyle believes that Jamie was pushed off that building. That he found out something was going on inside Wallace or Montgomery and he was killed to keep it quiet. So, I've taken a leave from my teaching job. I've canceled my plane reservations to go back to North Carolina for now. I know you won't fully understand, but this is what I need to do to finish this for Jamie. It's what I *can* do."

"And you are willing to put yourself in danger now? No! Hell no! Think of Natalie!"

"CJ, that's not fair. You know I always think of her first."

CJ moved closer to Hailey and stood directly in front of her. He lowered his voice to a whisper. "We've just found each other again. What about that? I won't be able to bear it if something happens to you."

She teased a piece of hair away from his forehead. "I can't bring him back. I can't fix the past. This, right here and now, is what I can do for him. I don't need your approval to do this, CJ. But I want your support."

"And if I can't give it to you? You'll do it anyway. And I'll lose you to Jamie again."

"I'm done waiting around. I'm done being the victim in my own life story. Lost homes, lost children, lost husbands."

"Why is it so hard, Hailey? Why can't we ever just be right? I waited for you so many years. I'm not going to wait around to watch you put yourself in danger. I'm done waiting, Hailey. I can't believe I'm saying this. I'm losing you again."

"You don't have to."

He walked away, leaving her standing alone in the room holding a glass of untouched Scotch.

Chapter 13

"AMY!!!" Natalie burst through the apartment's front door and landed on her aunt with a hug.

"Hi, bugaboo. What's up?" Amy set Natalie down to stand on the coffee table and turned to face Hailey, who'd followed her daughter into the apartment. "I'm so happy to see you at…" She leaned over to see the time on the microwave. "Six A.M."

"Sorry, love. We need to talk. Natalie, can you ask Aunt Amy if she has some crayons and paper? I need you to draw me a picture of home. I miss it." Hailey moved toward the kitchen to put down her purse.

"I don't have crayons, but I have ballpoint pens and highlighters. Will that work?"

Hailey started to push through the items in her enormous bag. "I might have some in here. Maybe not the best idea to give her permanent ink."

"I don't care. I'm fun Aunt Amy, and I rent." She walked over to her nightstand to find the pens and paper.

Giving up the search, Hailey bent down to her daughter's level. "Alright, baby. Try to stay on the paper. Aunt Amy and I have to talk for a bit."

"Oh, goodie." Amy walked to the front door and closed it before moving into the kitchen. "Hailey, it's six A.M. On Saturday, my only day off this week. Why are you here?"

Hailey hadn't been able to sleep after her fight with CJ. She had already called an unhappy Kyle and woken him up too. "I saw you last night. I talked to Kyle."

Amy pulled her head out of the refrigerator and peeked over the door. "Okay... I'm allowed to date now, you know. Is this about the other guy? Scott?"

"No… and yes."

"Oh, good. I see I'm gonna need coffee for this conversation. Do you want some?" Amy made a cup of coffee from the instant machine on her counter.

"Yes, the way things are going, make it a double." Hailey sat heavily on the kitchen chair and put her head on the table.

Amy plunked a hot mug of coffee in front of her sister. "Start with how you saw me last night and why you talked to Kyle."

"I'm going to have to start further back than that. You're not going to be happy when you hear it. I'm not looking forward to a lecture this morning. Remember, little ears may be listening." Hailey motioned toward Natalie, who was happily singing to herself and coloring her picture.

"Well, you'll get what you get. You're the one who woke me up this morning. Start talking." Amy wrapped her robe around her short pajamas and sat cross-legged on the chair opposite from Hailey. "Come on, rip off the Band-Aid. Let's hear it."

As quickly as she could, all in one big breath, Hailey spit it out. "I worked for the FBI, and Jamie knew about it, and he might have been murdered, and Kyle is in the FBI too, and you went on a date with him, so he doesn't want you to know anything, and I've agreed to help him figure out what happened, and CJ stomped out when I told him… "

"Wait, wait, wait. You were in the FBI? That is so cool!"

"Seriously, Amy, that is what you want to focus on here?"

"We'll get to the other stuff, but what the actual hell, Hailey? Did you carry a gun? Did you ever shoot anyone?"

Hailey put her finger to her mouth and leaned forward. "Shhh… Stop, Amy. It was not glamorous or special. I worked on computers and hacked code. I never carried a gun. I'm embarrassed to say I even did it."

"Embarrassed? To have helped fight crime and to have kept our country safe?"

Hailey sipped her coffee and stared across the steam at her little sister. "Jamie kept us safe. I just listened to phone calls and hacked a few systems."

"You really know how to do that? That's amazing. Knowing you, you were probably the director of the agency and just don't want to say so. And I know Kyle works for the FBI. He told me. He doesn't get involved with anyone unless they can handle the job. I think it's awesome. A little scary, yes, but still pretty damn cool. Did you know he speaks five languages?"

"Yes, I'm aware." Hailey rolled her eyes and laughed for the first time that day. Her heart was always a little lighter with Amy around.

"So, obviously, Jamie was pushed off that building. What are your leads?" Amy took an unapologetic slug of her coffee.

"What? That's it. I tell you I did this job, Jamie was killed, Kyle and I are working the case, and now you want to work it with me?"

"If I remember the whole sentence, you also said CJ stomped out, but we can deal with that later. He's not going anywhere. If you're in, he's in. Face it, sister, he's loved you for years. He's going to find a way to make this happen. No way he's losing you twice."

Hailey sat back in the chair with a small grunt. "I really don't have time to worry about CJ's ego right now. I have to keep you safe."

"Me? I'm perfectly safe. What are you talking about now?"

"Scott. I think he may be the one on the inside at Montgomery. Maybe even the one who killed Jamie. And I've set you up on a date with him tonight."

"Wow. You are extraordinarily bad at this matchmaking stuff." Amy laughed loudly.

"Shut up. But I can't let you go on this date, Amy. You have to call and cancel."

"Why? Maybe I can get some information for you. He'd never suspect. I'm just the little sister set-up. Does he know that you suspect anything?"

"No, I don't think so. There's no real investigation here. It's hunches and no backup. Except Kyle."

"That's my kind of backup." Amy winked at her sister. "If there's no investigation, then how much danger could I really be in? You could listen in and get me out if something sounds off." She smiled. "Secret Agent Amy has a nice ring to it."

"I can't let you. And I can't be there. One of the only clues I have says a ship is coming in tonight. I have no idea what is on it or why it is important, but I have to check it out. I'm going to try to look around Montgomery Shipping tonight and see what kind of documentation I can find in their system."

"So, danger is fine for you, but I should sit home and worry about you instead of helping? No way, sister. I'm in."

"I can't believe I am considering this. Am I considering this?"

Amy peeled a banana from the fruit bowl on the table. "It's done, sister. I'm supposed to meet Scott at the Upper Cut Chophouse at eight tonight. I'll talk to Kyle and throw him off the scent. If he thinks I'm seeing Scott, he won't be able to stay out of it."

Tapping her finger on table, Hailey considered the situation. "We'll need to find a way to have your phone on to record what he says. And I'm coming to pick you up at nine thirty, after I check out Montgomery. A nice boring hour and a half, and then you are out of there. Don't try to probe or provoke him, Amy."

"I'll do my best." Amy reached over to lay her hand on Hailey's. "We are going to figure this out for Jamie and for you. Time to clean this up and get on with your life."

"Here you go, Mommy." Natalie put a picture of their North Carolina home on the table in front of Hailey and climbed into Amy's lap. She took a bite of Amy's banana. "See, I put you and me right there. And that's CJ. And that's a flag for Daddy."

"Thank you, baby. It's perfect." Hailey looked up at the tears in her sister's eyes.

"We're gonna get you there."

Chapter 14

Montgomery Shipping was relatively easy to get into, especially with JP Montgomery's ID badge, which she'd borrowed earlier in the day. It was Saturday, so the odds were that JP wouldn't notice it was missing, and it would be back on his suit coat before morning. It was a risk, especially given his potential involvement in the situation.

She swiped the badge at the private elevator and took it to the eighteenth floor. One more swipe, through the large glass doors, and she was inside the Montgomery offices. Quiet cubicles, empty offices, with the light on in only one. Forgotten in the hurry out for the weekend. Off to drinks, and dates, and life.

She'd helped Amy earlier in the evening ready herself for her date with Scott and now was using his distraction to search the place. Worry riled up her stomach. Hives threatened. She told herself that she needed to finish this for Jamie. For Natalie too. Home was waiting.

She walked the length of the narrow hallway, running her hand across the nameplate on the door as she reached Scott's office. The door was open. She eased into his modern desk chair and started up the computer on the desk. Her knee bounced up and down while she waited. "Passcode? Passcode? Let's try Montgomery, shall we?

"And there we go. God, people are so predictable. How can they even consider that a level of security?" *Get it together girl. You are not here to improve their system. You're here to hack it.*

She started to work on the program recording ship logs, weights, and cargo. It appeared to be the source for the May 18th document Jamie had left in the safety deposit box at the bank. From the code, she could see that the information was entered at the port upon arrival. Montgomery worked electronically, with only a rare exception. Every document for a ship entering on Jamie's date list, however, was printed to a remote document station in the Wallace offices. And tonight's shipment had already been logged as well. "And what do we have here? A little ghost, eh? What are you trying to hide?" A ghost log-in had been used tonight to change the number of cargo containers logged, and the weight of the ship had been changed to reflect this subtraction. The document had been printed to the same document station inside Wallace.

Well, shit. She would have to risk entering the Wallace side of the offices. Perhaps whoever had printed the document hadn't picked it up yet.

JP's ID badge allowed her access to the security offices, reminding her that these two companies were linked. Anyone from either place could be responsible for Jamie's death, including JP. She moved quietly toward Mclanie's desk, figuring this was the hub of the office. She opened her low file drawer and started a quick manual search. Files were titled by date. May 18th was easy enough to find. She pulled the file and fingered through the pages for the document to match Jamie's. She took a picture on her phone and replaced the file.

As she moved to the copier, she noticed the paper jam light flashing in the dark. She pushed to clear the jam. No movement. She lifted the panel on the side to peek into the paper tray.

"You have to swear at it and hit the side pretty hard."

The hair on the back of her neck prickled. *Shit!* She spun around to see Matt standing several feet away.

She blew out a breath. "Oh, thank God it's you, Matt. You scared me."

"I scared you? No one's supposed to be here. What are you doing here, Hailey?"

"What are you doing here? I thought you were in North Carolina."

"I could say the same for you. Why are you snooping in here at this hour?"

"Uh… I was picking up some paperwork for Jamie's bank?" Her eyes darted to the gun resting in the holster on his right hip.

"Really? At nine o'clock on a Saturday night? In the dark…"

She was terrible at deceit. Always had been. "Okay, no, not really. Matt, I need your help." Her instincts told her to lie.

"What do you need? What is going on?" He moved a little closer and turned on the overhead lights.

"I'm not entirely sure." That part was true. The rest she would have to make up on the spot. "I think Jamie was doing something…

illegal. I don't know exactly what. I think it took his life. You were one of his oldest friends. Did you know what he was doing?"

"What did Jamie tell you?"

"Nothing. He didn't tell me anything. No one can tell me anything. Can you help me? What was he doing here?"

She moved away and sat at Melanie's pristine desk, putting some distance between herself and the gun she couldn't stop her eyes from returning to every other sentence. Her fingers shook, so she clasped her hands together.

"I don't know anything either, Hailey. Jamie was a boy scout. I doubt he was doing anything illegal. You've read too many spy novels. I came to finish my job on this shipment tonight." Matt hit the machine soundly, and the paper began to move. He signed the page and set it neatly in Melanie's inbox. "I just need to make a call to the port to let them know we are all set at this end. I'll be right back. Then we can go somewhere and talk if you want."

"Sure. Thanks, Matt, really."

She watched him walk away. He pulled out his cell and made the call. She overheard bits and pieces while she quickly took a photo of the document on her phone. "At the offices… It's complicated. Negative… Will do."

"All set?" She stood to leave. "I think I should get back home. I was silly for coming here. I'm sure Jamie would never do anything illegal."

"Do you want me to give you a ride home?" Matt placed his hand on her shoulder.

She jumped. *God, don't give yourself away now.* "No, thank you. I have a car. I just need a good night's sleep. I'm heading back to North Carolina soon. I hope I see you there."

"Sounds like a good plan."

She stepped back out of his grip and picked up her purse from the floor in front of the desk.

"What have you got in there?"

"Everything important, except Natalie." She smiled. And prayed he didn't read her too well. She pushed through the glass doors and into the elevator, texting Amy as she went.

Close call here. On my way to you.

She watched the blinking dots for a moment.

Good. I've stalled as long as possible.

Outside in 5

Hailey slipped into the borrowed Audi SUV and took her first deep breath. *Okay. That could have been worse.* She started the car and eased into Saturday downtown traffic. Within minutes, she felt her heart rate return to normal as she pulled into the valet lane at the Upper Cut. She watched Amy politely shake Scott's hand and move toward the car. She put down the window as her sister climbed into the passenger seat.

"Hi, Scott. Thanks for taking Amy out."

Her sister elbowed her ribs.

"I enjoyed it. Thanks for the set-up. You ladies be safe now on your way home. Goodnight, Amy." Scott waved and moved back onto the sidewalk as Hailey pulled away.

"Thank God you came to get me! No more set-ups, ever. I mean it, Hailey. I need to wash the ick off now. I kept thinking, this bastard killed Jamie, and now he wants to put his hand on my thigh. Who does that? Slime-y." Amy visibly shook from shoulders to hips.

"Did he say anything about Jamie? Anything helpful?"

"I doubt it. I was only half-listening after a while. This surveillance stuff is bor-ing."

Hailey peeked in her rearview mirror as a sedan pulled up behind her without its lights on. "My evening was less boring. Matt caught me at the offices."

"What? Really? What did you say?"

"I got a weird vibe from him. I tried to throw him off a bit. But something was off. Like this guy behind me, what is up with him?" She gently tapped the brakes to signal him to back off.

Amy looked in the side mirror. "He's pretty close to your bumper. Jerk. You want me to flip him off?"

"No. No, Amy. Jeez. I just hate Chicago traffic. And this investigation is making me paranoid. I'm sure it's fine. Tell me what you guys talked about."

"Not much. Growing up in Chicago. He's a Sox fan." Amy stuck her tongue out and pretended to gag herself. "He likes classical jazz, whatever that is, and enjoys art in any form." She put up air quotes around "in any form." "Damn, he never shut up about his collection of paintings except when he took, I kid you not, no less than seven phone calls during our date. He probably thinks I have some sort of bladder condition, as I excused myself no less than three times to use the restroom and get away from the table. Hey!" The car behind them rear ended them just enough to move them forward in traffic. "What the… "

"Well, maybe I'm not paranoid." Hailey took an opportunity to pull into the right lane and turned right at the next side street. The car behind followed. "Do you think we should stop?"

"Um, no. Hailey, this is definitely freaking me out. Drive back toward downtown. See if he follows." Hailey put on her blinker to move over a lane. "Well, don't use your signal. Jeez, car chase 101. I would have thought they taught that at FBI school."

"Shut up, Amy. Can you see the driver?"

"No, tinted windows and maybe a hat. I can't tell."

"Just one driver. Anyone in the passenger seat?" Hailey turned right at Lake Shore Drive.

"No, just the one guy. Move into the left lane there."

"I don't like this. He's backing off but still following us. I'm not dropping you off at your apartment."

"No. Not good. Should we head out to the Montgomerys'?" Amy was turned almost backward in her seat, watching through the rear window.

"No. Natalie is there. I'm not going to bring this anywhere near her. We've got to lose him. I'm going to try to get through this light…"

༄

"Mrs. Johnston? What are you doing in my hospital tonight?" CJ noted the muumuu choice today was green with bright-yellow sunflowers. It almost hurt his eyes. He turned to close the curtain separating them from other patients in the ER.

"Dr. Montgomery. I'm so glad you are on call. I missed you."

"I'm sure that's not why you came in tonight."

"No, but it's true. How have you been? You look like you haven't slept in days. You haven't shaved. Your hair needs a trim. You look like a man in love."

"I'm a man on call, Mrs. Johnston… And she has doubts." *How does this woman get me to talk about this stuff?* CJ sat on the round stool at the bedside.

"I'm so sorry." She reached out to rest her hand on his, patting it twice.

"You are very kind, Mrs. Johnston. What brings you in tonight?"

"Oh," she answered, as if she'd forgotten her real purpose or that it was just to check on him. "I think my diverticulitis is back. I finished my antibiotics last week, but I've had pain for twenty-four hours and fever tonight."

"Well, that's no good. Can I examine your belly?"

"Of course. Left side, about here." CJ very gently pressed on her upper stomach, then mid-left side, and then, finally, she winced as his hand pushed down on the left lower quadrant of her abdomen.

"That's the spot, huh? Okay. We'll get some labs and a CT, start some antibiotics, and see how things go."

A nurse pushed open the curtain enough to stick her head into the room. "Dr. Montgomery, MVA on its way in, thirties, white female, multiple injuries, trauma bay 1."

"I have to go, Mrs. Johnston. We'll get things started as soon as we can."

"Of course, transports me back to the field. I wish I could get off this gurney and lend a hand."

He put up his hand and smiled. "You stay put now. I'll be back."

CJ pulled the curtain closed behind him, fitted his surgical cap over his head and safety glasses onto his forehead, and stripped off his white coat. As he turned the corner toward the trauma bay, he saw her standing in the hallway, dazed, her shirt smeared with blood, skin pale as the moon.

"Hailey!" He caught her in his arms as her knees gave out. "Hailey! Where are you hurt?"

"Not me," she whispered. As she spoke, a gurney rushed past them. An EMT was performing chest compressions on top of the young woman covered in blood. "Amy…"

CJ pushed Hailey to sit by the wall, out of the way. Kyle ran in after her. CJ pointed at him. "Stay with her!"

"But Amy?" Hailey objected.

"I've got Amy. Stay with Kyle. Got it?" Hailey nodded her understanding while Kyle crouched to help her up. "Hailey, look at me! Are you sure you're not hurt?"

She nodded without looking at him. *That will have to do*, he thought. "I'm going to Amy now." His eyes shot up at Kyle, anger shaking inside of him. "Get her checked out. She's in shock. How could you let this happen?"

"Not the time, Dr. Montgomery! Go! I've got her."

He rushed to the room and quickly surveyed the scene. His room. His scene. Instinct kicked in. It was like a concert in his head, each movement in sync with the next, all the moving parts swaying with the rhythm. He'd trained his life for this. He'd given up his life for this.

The respiratory therapist squeezed the bag attached to the breathing tube to ventilate the patient. An emergency room technician cut Amy's clothes away. A nurse performed compressions. The emergency room physician – Dr. Daniels, he thought – was listening to Amy's chest. Blood oozed from a head laceration and dripped onto the trauma bed.

The paramedic's report cut through the other noise. "ET tube's in, but ventilating with difficulty. PEA on the monitor. Compressions ongoing. Abdominal distention, likely internal bleeding, chest contusion."

A nurse added, "Two IVs started, fluids open, type and cross is pending, but trauma blood is ready."

Dr. Daniels removed the stethoscope from his ears. "Right tension pneumothorax."

"Let's prep for a needle decompression." CJ gloved himself and cleaned the right chest quickly with some betadine. "Needle." A smooth push, a rush of air.

The respiratory therapist called out, "She's ventilating easier, Dr. Montgomery."

"What's the rhythm now?" CJ held his breath.

"Sinus tach."

"Do we have a pulse?"

"Yes, but it's thready. Checking BP."

CJ felt a surge of relief. *Thank God*, he thought. The nurse doing compressions climbed off the bed and backed away, catching his breath.

"BP's low but holding."

Dr. Daniels had pulled the ultrasound over and started an exam on Amy's abdomen. "We've got free fluid everywhere."

"Okay. Good work, team. Let's move her to the OR."

CJ rushed past Hailey, her head on Kyle's shoulder and tear stains washing the blood from her cheeks. "We're going to the OR. I've got her, Hailey. I've got her."

Chapter 15

Another hospital, another ICU, another damn metal chair… her only sister. Hailey held Amy's hand and rested her head on the mattress. *This is not happening again. I will not be another victim here.* Her thoughts were jumbled, much like her exact memories of the night's events.

"She's going to be fine, Hailey." CJ had walked in and stood next to her without her realizing he was there. He rested his hand on her back and gave a gentle rub. Before he could step back, she was in his arms, tears streaming.

"Thank you, CJ. Thank you for saving my sister." She held on for life.

"It's what we do. She's lucky to have you, lucky that you got her here so fast. Now, sit back down. I can only assume this accident had something to do with the investigation. Right?" She rested her forehead on her palms and let the tears fall to the floor. "Are you sure you're not hurt? Did you get checked out in the ER?"

"I'm fine."

"We've talked about that word, Hailey. No one is fine. Take me, for instance. I'm mad as hell. I'm frustrated." He knelt down to meet her at eye level. "I'm scared."

"I'm numb."

He put his hands on either side of her head and spoke directly. "Well, it's a start." He scanned the room. "Now, where is Kyle, and how should I dispose of his body?"

"I sent him out after the bad guys. None of this is his fault. He didn't know what we were doing."

"We? Amy was working with you on this? Jesus, Hailey. I can't fathom how that was a good idea." He pushed to a stand and started to check the IV bag hanging above Amy's bed.

"I had no choice. I never have with her. She's pushy and strong-willed... God, I need her to be strong-willed right now." Hailey grabbed her sister's hand again and resumed her vigil. "My stupid matchmaking got her into this. I set her up on a date before I even suspected Scott Cannon was part of this. Once she found out what was going on, there was no talking her out of it. She was all in. She always is."

"I know the feeling." He pulled up a chair next to her. "Tell me exactly what happened. No more secrets. How did Scott hurt Amy? I clearly don't understand."

Before she could answer, Kyle knocked on the ICU door and stepped inside.

The metal chair screeched across the floor as CJ jumped from his seat. "You fucking bastard! How could you pull these women into this? Where were you tonight while all this was going down?" CJ gripped Kyle's shirt and pushed him against the wall.

Hailey wedged herself between the men, her back to Kyle. She pressed her hand to CJ's chest. "Stop! Stop! CJ! I don't need you to do this. It was my choice. My job. My life!" CJ pushed away as she finished. "I've never had a choice. Can you see that? You were not an option. I got pregnant. Jamie left us. None of that was my choice. I was taking back my life tonight."

"But he let you endanger yourself! You're going to defend him?"

"No. This is not Kyle's fault. He didn't know what I was doing tonight. Amy went out to dinner with Scott to distract him. For me. She told Kyle she had canceled. She knew he wouldn't let her get involved."

Kyle sat in Hailey's chair and took Amy's hand. "Damn right. But I figured something was up. This is not my first rodeo. I followed her to the Upper Cut. Sat at the bar and tried to listen in on their conversation. Felt like a stalker. Except she'd have killed me if she'd seen me. I followed your car out and onto the street. I saw him rear-end you, and I watched the accident happen. Couldn't do anything to stop it. I called 911. I started CPR."

"Shit!" CJ visibly softened. "I'm sorry, Kyle. You did good to get her here so fast. She's gonna recover. You did that."

"Thanks, CJ. But you did that."

Hailey reached out to hold CJ's hand. She placed it over her heart, focused on only him while she asked Kyle the question holding her chest in a vice. "Kyle, did you get them?"

Relief flooded his face, and a sly smile emerged. "You bet your ass I did. We did."

CJ furrowed his brow at Hailey. "Who's them? How?"

Hailey smiled at the thought. She let go of CJ to move back to Amy's bedside. "I figured it out. I was just about an hour too late. Scott Cannon and Matt Callahan killed Jamie. They've been using Montgomery Shipping and Wallace Security to cover up their business of moving guns, drugs, hell… maybe even people, into the port on Montgomery ships. Jamie found out. He left me the clues, and tonight, I figured it out. Just an hour too late."

"But Scott has been with Montgomery for years. He's like part of the family. How long has this been going on? What kind of proof did you find?"

"While you were in surgery saving Amy, I put it together. I went to Montgomery Shipping tonight looking for answers while Amy had Scott out of the office, distracted. I needed to check on the ship and cargo that came in tonight. It was one of the dates on Jamie's list."

"That's where this started? How did you even get in?"

Hailey flushed with embarrassment. "I took your dad's ID badge from the house."

CJ laughed out loud. "Wow! You've got bigger balls than me. Can I be there when you return it and you tell him about the car? Jeez, Hailey."

"I broke into his computer system too."

"Shit! You know how to do that?"

She waved her hand in the air. "That was the easy stuff tonight. While I was inside, I found what I needed to take Scott down. I found a ghost. Jamie had left a single copy of a May 18th ledger in his safety deposit box. Weird, right? Why keep that specific page? That's what I went to find out. When I compared it, the paper version didn't match the one in the system. He'd been able to print it out before the ghost had changed it."

"What do you mean? What is a ghost?" CJ asked carefully.

"It's a coded sign-in without a traceable signature. A ghost can get in without being detected and change the data – to make guns, drugs, or people disappear. As if they had never arrived at all. Well, unless you know how to find him. Tonight's ship, too, had an electronic ledger, one that had already been changed. Someone printed it remotely to Wallace, and that's where Matt found me. I thought I threw him off, but my acting could probably use some work. He must have called Scott while he was on his date with Amy. Someone started following us. We tried to get away, but we got hit, T-boned on Amy's side, when I went through a red light."

"But…"

She interrupted him. "Nothing you can say will make me feel worse than I already do. So don't. Just don't."

"I was going to say, how is this evidence against Scott?"

"Now you sound like Kyle. The night I ran out of the bowling alley, I had finally figured out that Scott was involved. Things just didn't add up. CJ, you told me at dinner that Scott had never met Jamie, but the hot girl at the reception desk…"

"Katrina," both men said in unison.

Hailey rolled her eyes as the men chuckled. "Yes, the fair Katrina said Jamie waited for Scott often in the lobby and they would talk. I thought that was odd. Why deny that he knew Jamie? Then you said that thing about Kerry being JP's number two, and it finally dawned on me that the flash drive wasn't the second of two. The number two was the clue. It was a person. And on it was the link to Wallace."

"Wow. I thought medicine was complicated."

"The page on the drive, the one with all the ships' arrival dates, was copied with a skew, not straight. It came out of the Wallace copier, the one Melanie has to hit and curse at to get it to work. Jamie was leaving me another clue. Each of the dates on the page was a Montgomery ship, but the copy was made at Wallace's printer. Matt was in the office tonight to print the altered document because old man Wallace only works with paper."

"But how do you know Scott is the ghost? Matt could have called anyone in Montgomery tonight."

"I found Amy's phone. It got shoved into my purse at the accident scene. We'd rigged it to record their dinner conversation. Scott took the call at the table, while Amy was in the bathroom. If you listen, you can hear his half of the conversation. He told Matt to 'take care of them' and to make it look like an accident. That bastard smiled at us and told us to stay safe as he unleashed his dog on us. Jamie was on the right track, and he left me all the clues. He was a good man, a good soldier, and now he can finally rest."

Amy opened her eyes and scanned over to Kyle at her bedside. She whispered in her hoarse voice, "Did we get 'em?"

Kyle kissed her smartly. "Yes, ma'am. You bet your fine ass we did."

∞

The apartment was finally empty. Natalie slept on CJ's bed, her princess nightlight close by. Hailey lay quietly on the leather couch with her arm strewn over her eyes, processing the day. How could she process anything? How had she gotten here? Anywhere close to here?

Without actually seeing him, she knew CJ was there. She felt the couch bow as he sat at her feet, smelled the fresh scent of his body wash out of the shower, and relished the sweet release of tension as he began to massage her foot. "Can I get you something? Wine? Brandy?"

"That would require you to stop moving those magical hands that are currently my reason for living. No, you stay right where you are."

"Yes, ma'am."

Hailey giggled as CJ mocked her and Amy. "It's not fair. We get 'ma'am,' which makes us old hags with twenty-seven cats, and you guys get 'sir,' which makes you James Bond in a tuxedo."

"Ooh, say it again. I like the sound of it on your tongue."

Hailey sat up. She put on her best straight face and tormented him. "Sir, would you allow me to park your shiny German sports car? Sir?"

"No, but I'd like to take you for a ride." He moved so fast she never had time to react. His lips landed on her own, and he parted hers with his tongue and stoked the fire between them.

"CJ. We have to talk."

He pulled back and stared into her eyes. "You're not leaving. You're home."

"I've been struggling with that recently. Where is home? Not until tonight did I ever think it wasn't *where*, but *who*. You are my home. My heart is your heart. My pulse is your pulse. Why did it take us so long to get here? When we were teenagers, what held you back? You had so many opportunities to tell me. I was a puppy dog waiting to lap up any affection you might send my way. I need to know."

CJ pushed back to sit up on the couch. "I knew that you wanted to be my girlfriend. I always knew. I didn't want to… waste it. You were special. Not like Charlene Johnson, or Pam Clark, or…"

"Samantha Patterson…"

"Or Carrie Wilson…"

"Okay. I get it. You can stop now." She put her arm back over her eyes.

CJ pulled it back down. "My point is that I liked those girls but I knew they weren't the one. They weren't special enough to care how I spent the relationship. You were. I wanted to save that one chance with you. So I didn't screw it up. Until I looked around one day, and

Jamie had my girl. I was so damn afraid of using up my one chance with you that I lost my one chance with you."

"Well, then, I'm glad we get second chances."

She pulled him back down to taste his lips, to feel her own desire rise up.

"Hailey."

"Sir?"

"God, I want you. I've wanted you since I knew what it was to want anyone. I'll want you every day for the rest of my life. But I should ask what you want."

"Right now, after the events of the day, I want James Bond."

Epilogue

"Happy Birthday, Natalie!" Hailey and CJ stood next to each other while the princess greeted her royal subjects, otherwise known as the Montgomery family. Smiles, laughter, hope… Hailey was starting to feel it again after so many years.

Her baby turned five on this exceptionally mild, sunny mid-November day in Chicago, surrounded by everyone who loved her and dressed in glitter from head to toe. Jillian and Drew had kindly opened their home for the celebration, sharing their own joy with the family as it was now next to impossible to keep it in. Jillian was eighteen weeks pregnant.

After presents, Hailey watched Natalie chase the dog's ball across the yard in an attempt to get Drew's dog, D.C., to play along. He was having none of it from his bed on the deck, but Hailey could appreciate that Natalie was working off all her birthday energy. She'd sleep well tonight.

Hailey followed Jillian into the kitchen to cut the cake and get the gossip. "How is the pregnancy going, Jillian?" Amy joined them in the kitchen.

"I'm finally getting over the morning sickness, but I still can't make a pumpkin spice latte at work without throwing up. Shannon has taken over that duty. Good thing the season is almost over. Otherwise, I think it is going well."

Hailey smiled. "I'd say you glow, but I know I hated that when I was pregnant. It's sweat. That's the glow of pregnancy!"

The women laughed together as Natalie pulled on the bottom of her mom's shirt. Hailey picked her up and put her on her hip. "Hey, birthday girl. You worked up a sweat out there. Need something?"

Natalie reached out and rested her fingers on Jillian's belly. "Deuces."

"Aw, that's sweet, love. Jillian has a baby inside her tummy."

"Babies, Mama. Deuces."

Jillian appeared embarrassed. "Well…"

"What? Twins? You're kidding me, right?" Hailey and Amy looked at each other, shocked, and then let out a squeal each.

Natalie repeated herself. "I told you, Mama, deuces."

"Does anyone know, Jillian?" Hailey put down Natalie and gave Jillian a hug.

"Drew and I were keeping it a surprise. So, Miss Natalie, try to keep our secret. Okay?"

Natalie crossed her fingers over her mouth and threw away the key. Just then, CJ picked her up from behind and threw her over his shoulder. "What's all the squealing about over here?"

"Nothing, CJ!" Natalie smirked up at Jillian.

"Time for princess presents."

"I already opened my presents, silly goose."

He set her down and peered down into the biggest brown eyes. "Not the one from me. I'll meet you outside in five." CJ took Hailey's hand. "I need you outside too."

"I was going to help with cake distribution."

"It will have to wait. Come on." CJ pulled her away from the other women and walked with her across the house to the back door leading onto the deck. Most everyone was inside, visiting and enjoying the day. Molly and Sam played checkers on the floor in the living room. Kerry and Drew stood over them, critiquing the game from above. Andrea Montgomery sat next to her husband and laughed at a joke no one else heard.

Hailey laughed. "Where are we going?"

"I put the present out back. Natalie will need a little help opening it."

Outside, by the fence lined with trees and two Adirondack chairs, with the sun just beginning to descend, sat an enormous box wrapped in balloon paper. Natalie stood next to the box, head tilted back, in stunned silence.

"Is it for me, CJ? Can I open it?"

"Go on. It's your birthday."

With her mom's help, she lifted the lid of the box to find another smaller box inside. Then another, and another. Finally, she unwrapped a medium-sized box with two small ring boxes inside. One was labeled "Natalie." The other read Hailey's name.

"There's two, Mama!"

Hailey laughed but felt her stomach twist as well. "What is this about?"

"Natalie, open yours first." CJ sat in one of the chairs and put Natalie on his lap.

She popped open the small velvet jewelry box. "It's a ring."

"It's pink topaz. The color of your birthstone. I bought it to match your mama's."

"Thank you!" Natalie gave CJ a hug. "Open yours, Mama."

"Should I?" Hailey turned back toward the house, where everyone, including her parents, were lining the deck, smiling like fools. She looked into CJ's beautiful green eyes, knowing what was inside the box. It was a second chance.

It was a choice.

CJ knelt in front of her while Natalie clapped wildly. He took the box from her hand and opened it slowly. Inside, she saw a clear, round diamond with a sparkling pink topaz on either side. "Hailey Wilks Powers, I have loved you more days than not, near and far away, child and man. Love found its way back to this place. Will you choose me today? Tomorrow? And every day? Will you marry me?"

Tears sprang into Hailey's eyes. Happy tears. Joyful love. "We are a package deal. I have to ask Nat what she thinks."

Natalie jumped to her mom's side, hugged her leg, and put out two fingers toward CJ.

"I love you, CJ. Deuces."

About the Author

Jennifer Driscoll is an author, physician, keeper of sarcastic kids, and killer of house plants. She lives in beautiful Michigan with her family.

Like what you've read? Follow us on Facebook (@jenniferdriscollauthor) or Instagram (@iforgettherest) and spread the word to family and friends.

Looking for more Montgomery boys? Book 3 of the Chicago Series, Winters' Season, *follows the ever-steady Kerry as he seeks to go from friend to lover with a woman close to his heart but out of his reach.*

Winters' Season *coming soon.*